The **101** Dalmatians

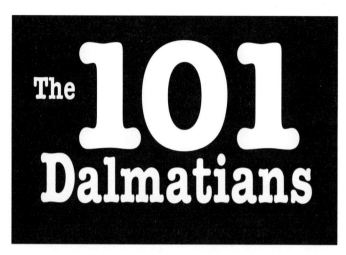

The 101 Dalmatians

The original novel by Dodie Smith

Illustrated by Michael Dooling

BARNES
&NOBLE
BOOKS
NEW YORK

First published in 1957 by Viking Penguin Inc.
Re-issued with illustrations by Michael Dooling in 1989

Copyright © Dodie Smith, 1956
Copyright renewed by Dodie Smith, 1984
Illustrations copyright © Viking Penguin Inc., 1989

THE HUNDRED AND ONE DALMATIANS appeared in serial form, with
different illustrations, as "The Great Dog Robbery," in WOMAN'S DAY.

This edition published by Barnes & Noble, Inc., by arrangement
with Viking Penguin, a division of Penguin Books USA, Inc.

1996 Barnes & Noble Books

ISBN 0-7607-0406-6

Printed and bound in the U.S.A.

96 97 98 99 00 M 9 8 7 6 5 4 3 2

FG

Contents

The 101 Dalmatians

The Happy Couples

Not long ago, there lived in London a young married couple of Dalmatian dogs named Pongo and Missis Pongo. (Missis had added Pongo's name to her own on their marriage, but was still called Missis by most people.) They were lucky enough to own a young married couple of humans named Mr. and Mrs. Dearly, who were gentle, obedient, and unusually intelligent—almost canine at times. They understood quite a number of barks: the barks for "Out, please!" "In, please!" "Hurry up with my dinner!" and "What about a walk?" And even when they could not understand, they could often guess—if looked at soulfully or scratched by an eager paw. Like many other much-loved humans, they believed that

3

they owned their dogs, instead of realizing that their dogs owned them. Pongo and Missis found this touching and amusing and let their pets think it was true.

Mr. Dearly, who had an office in the City, was particularly good at arithmetic. Many people called him a wizard of finance—which is not the same thing as a wizard of magic, though sometimes fairly similar. At the time when this story starts he was rather unusually rich for a rather unusual reason. He had done the Government a great service (something to do with getting rid of the national debt) and, as a reward, had been let off his income tax for life. Also the Government had lent him a small house on the Outer Circle of Regent's Park—just the right house for a man with a wife and dogs.

Before their marriages, Mr. Dearly and Pongo had lived in a bachelor flat, where they were looked after by Mr. Dearly's old nurse, Nanny Butler. Mrs. Dearly and Missis had also lived in a bachelor flat (there are no such things as spinster flats), where they were looked after by Mrs. Dearly's old nurse, Nanny Cook. The dogs and their pets met at the same time and shared a wonderfully happy double engagement, but they were all a little worried about what was to happen to Nanny Cook and Nanny Butler. It would be all right when the Dearlys started a family, particularly if it could be twins, with one twin for each Nanny, but until then, what were the Nannies going to do? For though they could cook breakfast and provide meals on trays (meals called "a nice egg by the fire") neither of them was capable of running a smart little house in Regent's Park, where the Dearlys hoped to invite their friends to dinner.

And then something happened. Nanny Cook and Nanny Butler met and, after a few minutes of deep suspicion, took a great liking to each other. And they had a good laugh about their names.

"What a pity we're not a real cook and butler," said Nanny Cook.

"Yes, that's what's needed now," said Nanny Butler.

And then they both together had the Great Idea: Nanny Cook would train to be a real cook and Nanny Butler would train to be a real butler. They would start the very next day and be fully trained by the wedding.

But you'll have to be a parlourmaid, really," said Nanny Cook.

"Certainly not," said Nanny Butler. "I haven't the figure for it. I shall be a real butler—*and* I shall valet Mr. Dearly, which will need no training as I've done it since the day he was born."

And so when the Dearlys and the Pongos got back from their joint honeymoon, there were Nanny Cook and Nanny Butler, fully trained, ready to welcome them into the little house facing Regent's Park.

It came as something of a shock that Nanny Butler was wearing trousers.

"Wouldn't a black dress with a nice frilly apron be better?" suggested Mrs. Dearly—rather nervously, because Nanny Butler had never been *her* Nanny.

"You can't be a butler without trousers," said Nanny Butler firmly. "But I'll get a frilly apron tomorrow. It will add a note of originality." It did.

The Nannies said they no longer expected to be called Nanny, and were now prepared to be called by their surnames, in the correct way. But though you can call a cook "Cook," the one thing you cannot call a butler is "Butler," so in the end both Nannies were just called "Nanny, darling," as they always had been.

After the dogs and the Dearlys had been back from their honeymoons for several happy weeks, something even happier happened. Mrs. Dearly took Pongo and Missis across the park to St. John's Wood, where they called on their good friend, the Splendid Veterinary Surgeon. She came back with the wonderful news that the Pongos were shortly to become parents. Puppies were due in a month.

The Nannies gave Missis a big lunch to keep her strength up, and Pongo a big lunch in case he should feel neglected (as the fathers of expected puppies sometimes do), and then both dogs had a long afternoon nap on the best sofa. By the time Mr. Dearly came home from business they were wide awake and asking for a walk.

"Let us *all* go for a walk, to celebrate," said Mr. Dearly, after hearing the good news. Nanny Cook said the dinner was well ahead, and Nanny Butler said she could do with a bit of exercise, so off they all set along the Outer Circle.

The Dearlys led the way, Mrs. Dearly very pretty in the green going-away suit from her trousseau, and Mr. Dearly in his old tweed jacket, which was known as his dog-walker. (Mr. Dearly wasn't exactly handsome, but he had the kind of face you don't get tired of.) Then came the Pongos, looking noble; they could both have become champions if Mr. Dearly had not felt that dog shows would bore them—and him. They had splendid heads, fine shoulders, strong legs, and straight tails. The spots on their bodies were jet-black and mostly the size of a two-shilling piece; they had smaller spots on their heads,

legs, and tails. Their noses and eye-rims were black. Missis had a most winning expression. Pongo, though a dog born to command, had a twinkle in his eye. They walked side by side with great dignity, only putting the Dearlys on the leash to lead them over crossings. Nanny Cook (plump) in her white overall, and Nanny Butler (plumper) in a well-cut tail coat and trousers, plus dainty apron, completed the procession.

It was a beautiful September evening, windless, very peaceful. The park and the old, cream-painted houses facing it basked in the golden light of sunset. There were many sounds but no noises. The cries of playing children and the whir of London's traffic seemed quieter than usual, as if softened by the evening's gentleness. Birds were singing their last song of the day, and farther along the Circle, at the house where a great composer lived, someone was playing the piano.

"I shall always remember this happy walk," said Mr. Dearly.

At that moment the peace was shattered by an extremely strident motor horn. A large car was coming towards them. It drew up at a big house just ahead of them, and a tall woman came out onto the front-door steps. She was wearing a tight-fitting emerald satin dress, several ropes of rubies, and an absolutely simple white mink cloak, which reached to the high heels of her ruby-red shoes. She had a dark skin, black eyes with a tinge of red in them, and a very pointed nose. Her hair was parted severely down the middle and one half of it was black and the other white—rather unusual.

"Why, that's Cruella de Vil," said Mrs. Dearly. "We were at school together. She was expelled for drinking ink."

"Isn't she a bit showy?" said Mr. Dearly, and would have turned back. But the tall woman had seen Mrs. Dearly and come down the steps to meet her. So Mrs. Dearly had to introduce Mr. Dearly.

"Come in and meet *my* husband," said the tall woman.

"But you were going out," said Mrs. Dearly, looking at the chauffeur who was waiting at the open door of the large car. It was painted black and white, in stripes—rather noticeable.

"No hurry at all. I insist on your coming."

The Nannies said they would get back and see about dinner, and take the dogs with them, but the tall woman said the dogs must come in too. "They are so beautiful. I want my husand to see them," she said.

"What is your married name, Cruella?" asked Mrs. Dearly, as they walked through a green marble hall into a red marble drawing room.

"My name is still de Vil," said Cruella. "I am the last of my family so I made my husband change his name to mine."

Just then the absolutely simple white mink cloak slipped from her shoulders to the floor. Mr. Dearly picked it up.

"What a beautiful cloak," he said. "But you'll find it too warm for this evening."

"I never find anything too warm," said Cruella. "I wear furs all the year round. I sleep between ermine sheets."

"How nice," said Mrs. Dearly politely. "Do they wash well?"

Cruella did not seem to hear this. She went on, "I worship furs, I live for furs! That's why I married a furrier."

Then Mr. De Vil came in. He was a small, worried-looking man who didn't seem to be anything besides a furrier. Cruella introduced him and then said, "Where are those two delightful dogs?"

Pongo and Missis were sitting under the grand piano, feeling hungry. The red marble walls had made them think of slabs of raw meat.

"They're expecting puppies," said Mrs. Dearly happily.

"Oh, are they? Good!" said Cruella. "Come here, dogs!"

Pongo and Misses came forward politely.

"Wouldn't they make enchanting fur coats?" said Cruella to her husband. "For spring wear, over a black suit. We've never thought of making coats out of dogs' skins."

Pongo gave a sharp, menacing bark.

"It was only a joke, dear Pongo," said Mrs. Dearly, patting him. Then she said to Cruella, "I sometimes think they understand every word we say."

But she did not really think it. And it was true.

That is, it was true of Pongo. Missis did not understand quite so many human words as he did. But she understood Cruella's joke and thought it a very bad one. As for Pongo, he was furious. What a thing to say in front of his wife when she was expecting her first puppies! He was glad to see Missis was not upset.

"You must dine with us—next Saturday," said Cruella to Mrs. Dearly.

And as Mrs. Dearly could not think of a good excuse (she was very truthful) she accepted. Then she said they must not keep the de Vils any longer.

As they went through the hall, a most beautiful white Persian cat dashed past them and ran upstairs. Mrs. Dearly admired it.

"I don't like her much," said Cruella. "I'd drown her if she wasn't so valuable.

10

The cat turned on the stairs and made an angry spitting noise. It might have been at Pongo and Missis—but then again, it might not.

"I want you to hear my new motor horn," said Cruella as they all went down the front-door steps. "It's the loudest horn in England."

She pushed past the chauffeur and sounded the horn herself, making it last a long time. Pongo and Missis were nearly deafened.

"Lovely, lovely dogs," Cruella said to them as she got into the striped black-and-white car. "You'd go so well with my car—and my black-and-white hair."

Then the chauffeur spread a sable rug over the de Vils' knees and drove the striped car away.

"That car looks like a moving Zebra Crossing," said Mr. Dearly. "Was your friend's hair black-and-white when she was at school?"

"She was no friend of mine, I was scared of her," said Mrs. Dearly. "Yes, her hair was just the same. She had one white plait and one black."

Mr. Dearly thought how lucky he was to be married to Mrs. Dearly and not to Cruella de Vil. He felt sorry for her husband. Pongo and Missis felt sorry for her white cat.

The golden sunset had gone now, and the blue twilight had come. The park was nearly empty, and a park-keeper was calling, "All out, all out!" in a far away voice. There was a faint scent of hay from the sun-scorched lawns, and a weedy, watery smell from the lake. All the houses on the Outer Circle that had been turned into government offices were now closed for the night. No light shone in their windows. But the Dearlys

11

could see welcoming lights in their own windows. And soon Pongo and Missis sniffed an exquisite smell of dinner. The Dearlys liked it too.

They all paused to look down through the iron railings at the kitchen. Although it was in the basement, this was not at all a dark kitchen. It had a door and two large windows opening onto one of the narrow paved yards which are so often found in front of old London houses. The correct name for these little basement yards is "the area." A narrow flight of steps led up from the area to the street.

The Dearlys and the dogs thought how very nice their brightly lit kitchen looked. It had white walls, red linoleum, and a dresser on which was blue-spotted china. There was a new-fashioned electric stove for the cooking, and an old-fashioned kitchen fire to keep the Nannies happy. Nanny Cook was basting something in the oven, while Nanny Butler stacked plates on the lift which would take them up through the dining-room floor as if delivering the Demon King in a pantomime. Near the fire were two cushioned dog-baskets. And already two superb dinners, in shining bowls, were waiting for Pongo and Missis.

"I hope we haven't tired Missis," said Mr. Dearly as he opened the front door with his latch-key.

Missis would have liked to say she had never felt better in her life. As she could not speak, she tried to *show* how well she felt, and rushed down to the kitchen, lashing her tail. So did Pongo, looking forward to his dinner and a long, firelit snooze beside his dear Missis.

"I wish *we* had tails to wag," said Mr. Dearly.

The Puppies Arrive

CRUELLA DE VIL'S dinner party took place in a room with black marble walls, on a white marble table. The food was rather unusual.

The soup was dark purple. And what did it taste of? Pepper!

The fish was bright green. And what did *it* taste of? Pepper!

The meat was pale blue. And what did *that* taste of? Pepper!

Everything tasted of pepper, even the ice cream—which was black.

There were no other guests. After dinner, Mr. and Mrs. Dearly sat panting in the red marble drawing room, where an enormous fire was now burning. Mr. de Vil panted quite a bit too. Cruella, who was wearing a ruby satin dress with ropes of emeralds, got as close to the fire as she could.

"Make it blaze for me," she said to Mr. de Vil.

Mr. de Vil made such a blaze that the Dearlys thought the chimney would catch fire.

"Lovely, lovely!" said Cruella, clapping her hands with delight. "Ah, but the flames never last long enough!" The minute they died down a little, she shivered and huddled herself in her absolutely simple white mink cloak.

Mr. and Mrs. Dearly left as early as they felt was polite, and walked along the Outer Circle, trying to get cool.

"What a strange name 'de Vil' is," said Mr. Dearly. "If you put the two words together, they make 'devil.' Perhaps Cruella's a lady-devil. Perhaps that's why she likes things so hot!"

Mrs. Dearly smiled, for she knew he was only joking. Then she said, "Oh, dear! As we've dined with them, we must ask them to dine with us. And there are some other people we ought to ask. We'd better get it over before Missis has her puppies. Good gracious, what's that?"

Something soft was rubbing against her ankles.

"It's Cruella's cat," said Mr. Dearly. "Go home, cat. You'll get lost."

But the cat followed them all the way to their house.

"Perhaps she's hungry," said Mrs. Dearly.

"Very probably, unless she likes pepper," said Mr. Dearly. He was still gulping the night air to cool his throat.

"You stroke her while I get her some food," said Mrs. Dearly. And she went down the area steps and into the kitchen on tiptoe, so as not to wake Pongo and Missis, who were asleep in their baskets. Soon she came up with some milk and half a tin of sardines. The white cat accepted both, then began to walk down the area steps.

"Does she want to live with us?" said Mrs. Dearly.

It seemed as if the white cat did. But just then Pongo woke up and barked loudly. The white cat turned and walked away into the night.

"Just as well," said Mr. Dearly. "Cruella would have the law on us if we took her valuable cat."

Then they went down into the kitchen to receive the full force of Pongo's welcome. Missis, though sleepy, was fairly formidable too. There was a whirling mass of humans and dogs on the kitchen hearthrug—until Mrs. Dearly remembered, far too late, that Mr. Dearly's dress suit would be covered with white hairs.

It must have been about three weeks later that Missis began to behave in a very peculiar manner. She explored every inch of the house, paying particular attention to cupboards and boxes. And the place that interested her most was a large cupboard just outside the Dearlys' bedroom. The Nannies kept various buckets and brooms in this cupboard, and there wasn't a spare inch of space. Every time Missis managed to get in, she knocked something over with a clatter and then looked very ill-treated.

"Bless me, she wants to have her puppies there," said Nanny Cook.

"Not in that dark, stuffy cupboard, Missis, love," said Nanny Butler. "You need light and air."

But when Mrs. Dearly consulted the Splendid Veterinary Surgeon, he said what Missis needed most was a small, enclosed place where she would feel safe, and if she fancied the broom cupboard, the broom cupboard she'd better have. And she'd better have it at once and get used to it—even though the puppies were not expected for some days.

So out came the brooms and buckets and in went Missis, to her great satisfaction. Pongo was a little hurt that he was not allowed to go with her, but Missis explained to him that mother dogs like to be by themselves when puppies are expected, so he licked his wife's ear tenderly and said he quite understood.

"I hope the dinner party won't upset Missis," said Mr. Dearly, when he came home and found Missis settled in the cupboard. "I shall be glad when it's over."

It was to be that very night. As there were quite a lot of guests, the food had to be normal, but Mrs. Dearly kindly put tall pepper-grinders in front of the de Vils. Cruella ground so much pepper that most of the guests were sneezing, but Mr. de Vil used no pepper at all. And he ate much more than in his own house.

Cruella was busy peppering her fruit salad when Nanny Butler came in and whispered to Mrs. Dearly. Mrs. Dearly looked startled, asked the guests to excuse her, and hurried out. A few minutes later Nanny Butler came in again and whispered to Mr. Dearly. *He* looked startled, excused himself, and hurried out. Those guests who were not sneezing made polite conversation. Then Nanny Butler came in again.

"Ladies and gentlemen," she said dramatically, "puppies are arriving earlier than expected. Mr. and Mrs. Dearly ask you to remember that Missis has never before been a mother. She needs absolute quiet."

There was an instant silence, broken only by a stifled sneeze.

Then the guests rose, drank a whispered toast to the young mother, and tiptoed from the house.

All except Cruella de Vil. When she reached the hall she went straight to Nanny Butler, who was seeing the guests out, and demanded, "Where *are* those puppies?"

Nanny Butler had no intention of telling, but Cruella heard the Dearlys' voices and ran upstairs. This time she was wearing a black satin dress with ropes of pearls, but the same absolutely simple white mink cloak. She had kept it round her all through dinner, although the room was very warm (and the pepper very hot).

"I must, I must see the darling puppies," she cried.

The cupboard door was a little open. The Dearlys were inside, soothing Missis. Three puppies had been born before Nanny Butler, on bringing Missis a nourishing chicken dinner, had discovered what was happening.

Cruella flung open the door and stared down at the three puppies.

"But they're mongrels—all white, no spots at all!" she cried. "You must drown them at once."

Dalmatians are always born white," said Mr. Dearly, glaring at Cruella. "The spots come later."

"And we wouldn't drown them even if they *were* mongrels," said Mrs. Dearly indignantly.

"It'd be quite easy," said Cruella. "I've drowned dozens and dozens of my cat's kittens. She always chooses some wretched alley-cat for their father, so they're never worth keeping."

"Surely you leave her *one* kitten?" said Mrs. Dearly.

"If I'd done that, I'd be overrun with cats," said Cruella.

17

"Are you sure those horrid little white rats are pure Dalmatian puppies?"

"Quite sure," snapped Mr. Dearly. "Now please go away. You're upsetting Missis."

And indeed Missis was upset. Even with the Dearlys there to protect her and her puppies, she was a little afraid of this tall woman with black-and-white hair who stared so hard. And that poor cat who had lost all those kittens! Never, never, would Missis forget that! (And one day she was to be glad that she remembered it.)

"How long will it be before the puppies are old enough to leave their mother?" asked Cruella. "In case I want to buy some."

"Seven or eight weeks," said Mr. Dearly. "But there won't be any for sale." Then he shut the cupboard door in Cruella's face, and Nanny Butler firmly showed her out of the house.

Nanny Cook was busy telephoning the Splendid Vet, but he was out on another case. His wife said she would tell him as soon as he came home and there was no need to worry— it sounded as if Missis was getting on very well.

She certainly was. There was now a fourth puppy. Missis washed it, and then Mr. Dearly dried it, while Mrs. Dearly gave Missis a drink of warm milk. Then the pup was put with the other three, in a basket placed where Missis could see it. Soon she had a fifth puppy. Then a sixth—and a seventh.

The night wore on. Eight puppies, nine puppies! Surely that would be all? Dalmatians do not often have more in their first family. Ten puppies! Eleven puppies!

Then the twelfth arrived, and it did not look like its brothers and sisters. The flesh showing through its white hair was not

19

a healthy pink but a sickly yellow. And instead of kicking its little legs, it lay quite still. The Nannies, who were sitting just outside the cupboard, told Mr. and Mrs. Dearly that it had been born dead.

"But with so many, its mother will never miss it," said Nanny Cook comfortingly.

Mr. Dearly held the tiny creature in the palm of his hand and looked at it sorrowfully.

"It isn't fair it should have no life at all," said Mrs. Dearly with tears in her eyes.

Something he had once read came back to Mr. Dearly. He began to massage the puppy; then he tousled it gently in a towel. And suddenly there was a faint hint of pink around its nose—and then its whole little body was flushed with pink, beneath its snowy hair. Its legs moved! Its mouth opened! It was alive!

Mr. Dearly quickly put it close to Missis so that she could give it some milk at once, and it stayed there, feeding, until the next puppy arrived—for arrive it did. That made thirteen!

Shortly before dawn, the front doorbell rang. It was the Splendid Vet, who had been up all night saving the life of a dog that had been run over. By then all the puppies had been born, and Missis was giving breakfast to eight of them—all she could manage at one time.

"Excellent!" said the Splendid Vet. "A really magnificent family. And how is the father bearing up?"

The Dearlys felt guilty. They had not given Pongo a thought since the puppies had begun to arrive. He had been shut up in the kitchen. All night long he had paced backwards and forwards, and only once had he heard any news—when Nanny

20

Cook had come down to make coffee and sandwiches. She had told him that Missis was doing well—but only as a joke, for she had no idea he would understand.

"Poor Pongo, we must have him up," said Mrs. Dearly. But the Splendid Vet said mother dogs did not usually like to have father dogs around when puppies had just been born. At that moment there was a clatter of toenails on the polished floor of the hall—and upstairs, four at a time, came Pongo. Nanny Cook had just gone down to make some tea for the Splendid Vet, and the anxious father had streaked past her the minute she opened the kitchen door.

"Careful, Pongo!" said the Splendid Vet. "She may not want you."

But Missis was weakly thumping her tail. "Go down and have your breakfast and a good sleep," she said—but nobody except Pongo heard a sound. His eyes and his wildly wagging tail told her all he was feeling, his love for her and those eight fine pups enjoying their first breakfast. And those others, in the basket, waiting their turn—*how* many were there?

"It's a pity dogs can't count," said Mrs. Dearly.

But Pongo could count perfectly. He went downstairs with his head high and a new light in his fine dark eyes. For he knew himself to be the proud father of fifteen.

Perdita

"AND NOW," said the Splendid Vet to the Dearlys, "you must get a foster mother."

He explained that though Missis would do her best to feed fifteen puppies, doing so would make her terribly thin and tired. And the strong puppies would get more milk than the weak ones. The puppy Mr. Dearly had brought to life was very small and would need special care.

The largest pup of all had a black patch all over its ear and one side of its face. This is a bad fault in a Dalmatian—which should be born pure white, as Mr. Dearly had told Cruella de Vil. Some people *would* have drowned this patched pup, because it would never be valuable. But the Dearlys felt particularly fond of it because it had started life with a bit of bad

22

luck. (And they liked being able to recognize it. Until the spots started to come through, some weeks later, the big puppy with the patch and the small, delicate puppy were the only ones who could be told apart from the others.)

The Splendid Vet said the foster mother would have to be some poor dog who had lost her own puppies but still had milk to give. He thought he could get such a dog. But as he wasn't sure, the Dearlys had better telephone all the Lost Dogs' Homes. And until the foster mother was found, they could help Missis by feeding the pups with a doll's feeding bottle or an old-fashioned fountain-pen filler.

Then the Splendid Vet went home for an hour's sleep before starting his day's work.

Nanny Cook got breakfast, and Nanny Butler took Pongo for a run. And Missis was persuaded to leave her family for a few minutes' walk. When she came back, Mrs. Dearly had tidied the cupboard. Missis gave the second lot of pups a meal, and then she and her family of fifteen had a glorious sleep. And Pongo, down in the kitchen, had a glorious sleep too, knowing that all was well.

As soon as the shops opened, Mrs. Dearly went out and bought a doll's feeding bottle and a fountain-pen filler. And then Mr. Dearly and the Nannies took turns at feeding puppies. Mrs. Dearly fancied this job herself but was busy telephoning, trying to find a foster mother. The Nannies were too fat to be comfortable in the cupboard, so soon Mr. Dearly got the feeding job all to himself and became very good at it and just a bit bossy. Of course he couldn't go to business, which was awkward as he had an important business deal on.

Luckily there was a telephone in the Dearlys' bedroom and

it had a long cord to it. So Mr. Dearly was able to telephone while he was feeding the pups. There he was, in a dark cupboard with Missis, fifteen puppies, and the telephone. He nearly upset his important business deal by holding a pup to his ear and giving the telephone a drink of milk.

No sooner had Mr. Dearly put the telephone down than the Splendid Vet rang up to say he had not been able to find a foster mother. Neither had Mrs. Dearly, anywhere in London. She now started to ring up Lost Dogs' Homes outside London. It was late afternoon before she heard of a mother dog with some milk to give, nearly thirty miles from London. And this dog had only just been brought in and would have to be kept some days in case she was claimed.

Mr. Dearly put his head out of the cupboard. After being up all night and feeding pups all day, he was beginning to feel pretty tired, but he was determined to go on helping Missis until the foster mother arrived. "Why not go and see if you can *borrow* that dog?" he said. "Say we'll give it back if its owner turns up."

So Mrs. Dearly got the car from the old stable at the back of the house and drove off hopefully. But when she got to the Dogs' Home she found that the mother dog had already been claimed. She was glad for the dog's sake, but terribly disappointed. She thought of poor Missis getting exhausted by too many puppies, and of Mr. Dearly, who might easily refuse to come out of the cupboard for a good night's sleep, and she began to think she never *would* find a foster mother.

It was now almost dark, a gloomy, wet October evening. It had been raining all afternoon, but Mrs. Dearly hadn't minded when she was feeling hopeful. Now, as she started back for

24

London, the weather made her feel more and more depressed. And the rain got so heavy that the windscreen-wiper could hardly keep pace with it.

She was driving across a lonely stretch of common when she saw what looked like a bundle lying in the road ahead of her. She slowed down, and as she drew closer she saw that it was not a bundle but a dog. Instantly she thought it must have been run over. Dreading what she might find, she stopped the car and got out.

At first she thought the dog was dead, but as she bent down it struggled to its feet, showing no signs of injury. It was so plastered with mud that she could not see what kind of dog it was. What she *could* see, by the light from the car's headlights, was the poor creature's pitiful thinness. She spoke to it gently. Its drooping tail gave a feeble flick, then drooped again.

"I can't leave it here," thought Mrs. Dearly. "Even if it hasn't been run over, it must be near starvation. Oh, dear!" With seventeen dogs at home already, she had no wish to take back a stray, but she knew she would never bring herself just to hand this poor thing in at a police station.

She patted it and tried to get it to follow her. It was willing to, but its legs were so wobbly that she picked it up and carried it. It felt like a sack of bones. And as she noticed this, she also noticed something else. Hurriedly she laid the dog on the seat of the car, on a rug, and turned on the light. Then she saw that this was a mother dog and that in spite of its starving condition it still had some milk to give.

She sprang into the car and drove as fast as she safely could. Quite soon she was in the London suburbs. She knew it would still take her some time to get home, because of the traffic,

25

so she stopped at a little restaurant. Here the owner let her buy some milk and some cold meat and lent her his own dog's dishes. The starving dog ate and drank ravenously, then at once settled to sleep. The nice owner of the restaurant took back his dishes and wished Mrs. Dearly luck as she drove away.

She got home just as the Splendid Vet was arriving to see Missis and the puppies. He carried the stray dog in and down to the warm kitchen. After a careful examination he said he thought her thinness was due more to having had puppies than to long starvation and that, if she was fed well, the milk intended for her own puppies might continue. He guessed they had been taken away from her and she had got lost looking for them.

"She ought to have a bath," said Nanny Cook, "or she'll give our puppies fleas."

The Splendid Vet said a bath was a good idea, so the dog was carried into a little room which had been fitted up as a laundry. Nanny Cook got on with the bath as fast as she could because she was afraid Mr. Dearly might want to do the job himself. Mrs. Dearly had gone upstairs to tell him what was happening.

The stray seemed delighted with the warm water. She had just been covered with soap when Pongo came back from a walk with Nanny Butler and ran through the open door of the laundry.

"He won't hurt a lady," said the Splendid Vet.

"I should hope not, when she's going to help nurse his puppies," said Nanny Cook.

Pongo stood on his hind legs and kissed the wet dog on the

nose, telling her how glad he was to see her and how grateful his wife would be. (But no human heard him.) The stray said, "Well, I'll do my best, but I can't promise anything." (No human heard that, either.)

Just then Mr. Dearly came hurrying in to see the new arrival.

"What kind of dog is she?" he asked.

At that moment Nanny Cook began to rinse off the soap—and everyone gave a gasp. This dog was a Dalmatian too! But her spots, instead of being black, were brown—which in Dalmatians is called not "brown" but "liver."

"Eighteen Dalmatians under one roof," said Mr. Dearly gloatingly. "Couldn't be better." (But it could, as he was one day to learn.)

Wet, the poor liver-spotted dog looked thinner than ever.

"We'll call her Perdita," said Mrs. Dearly, and explained to the Nannies that this was after a character in Shakespeare. "*She* was lost. And the Latin word for lost is *perditus*." Then she patted Pongo, who was looking particularly intelligent, and said anyone would think he understood. And indeed he did. For though he had very little Latin beyond "*Cave canem*," he had, as a young dog, devoured Shakespeare (in a tasty leather binding).

Perdita was dried in front of the kitchen fire and given another meal. The Splendid Vet said she ought to start mothering puppies as soon as possible, to encourage her to provide more milk, so after she was quite dry and had taken a nap, two puppies were removed from the cupboard while Missis went out for a little air. The Splendid Vet said she would not know they had gone—which is possible, as she could not count as well as Pongo could. But she knew all about those puppies going because Pongo had told her and she had sent polite messages to Perdita. Missis felt a bit unhappy about giving any puppies up, but she knew it was for their good.

Before leaving, the Splendid Vet warned the Dearlys that if Perdita could not feed the puppies they must not be returned to Missis, for her sense of smell would tell her that they had been with some other dog and she might turn against them. And this does happen with some dogs. It would never have happened with Missis, but it will already have been seen that she and Pongo were rather unusual dogs. And so was Perdita. And so, if people only realized it, are many dogs. In fact, usual dogs are really more unusual than unusual dogs.

Anyway, Perdita was able to feed the two puppies. Pongo went upstairs and told Missis so (though to the Dearlys it only sounded like the thumping of his tail). Then he said good night and went back to the kitchen, where his basket was ready for him. Perdita had the basket Missis usually slept in. She had fed and washed the two puppies and was now having a light supper. (The Splendid Vet had said she must eat all she possibly could, to get her strength back.) Pongo had a snack himself, to encourage her. Then the Nannies went to bed and the kitchen was left in darkness except for the glow from the fire. And when the two puppies were asleep, Perdita told Pongo her story.

She had been born in a large country house, not far from the common where Mrs. Dearly had found her. Although very pretty, she had been less valuable than her brothers and sisters; her spots were rather small and her tail inclined to curl (it had straightened as she grew older). As no one rich or important wanted to be her pet, she was given to a farmer, who, though not cruel to her, never gave her the love all Dalmatians need. And he let her run wild, which is not good for any kind of dog.

A time came when she felt a great desire to marry. But no marriage was arranged for her and, as the farm was over a mile from any village, no dog had come courting her. So one day she set out to find a husband for herself.

Her way to the village lay across the common, where she saw a large, handsome car which had been driven onto the grass. A group of people were having a picnic—and with them was a superb liver-spotted Dalmatian. Now, liver-spotted Dalmatians are unusual. Perdita had been the only one in her family, and always thought herself a freak. She instantly knew that the dog on the common was no freak but a most valuable animal, for he wore a magnificent collar and was being offered a piece of chicken by a richly dressed lady. At that moment, he saw Perdita.

It was love at first sight. Without even bothering to eat the chicken, he came bounding to her, and they were away into a wood together before anyone could stop them. Here they made swift arrangements for their marriage, promising to love each other always. Then the happy husband told his wife she must, of course, come and live with him, and led her back to the common. But as they reached it, along came the farmer Perdita lived with, in his rattling old car. He dragged her into it—and the picnic party bundled her husband into their car. Both dogs struggled and howled but it was useless. The cars drove off in opposite directions.

Nine weeks after her marriage, Perdita had eight puppies.

The farmer did not give her extra food, or help to feed the puppies himself, so she got thinner and thinner; by the time her family was a month old, she was just skin and bone. Then the farmer put down some food for the puppies to eat, and they quickly learned how to, but they still went on taking all the milk Perdita could give them, so she never had a chance to regain her weight. She was such a very young mother, barely full-grown herself, but she loved her babies dearly and did all she could for them. And as she got thinner, they got fatter.

The spots on Dalmatians begin to come through after two weeks. But the time Perdita's family were six weeks old it was obvious that they were going to be beautifully marked and very valuable—Perdita heard the farmer say so to a stranger who came to the farm one morning. She was still helping to feed them; they would eat all the farmer offered and then come to her for milk. Then she and they would all have a happy sleep in the old box she had been given for a bed.

One afternoon she woke to find not one puppy in bed with her. She searched the farmhouse, she searched the farmyard. No puppies anywhere. She ran onto the road, fearing they might have been run over. On and on she went, pausing every few minutes to bark. No answering puppy-bark came to her. Soon it began to rain. She thought of the puppies all getting wet, and barked more and more desperately. A car nearly ran over her; she saved herself only by jumping into a muddy ditch, where the mud even got into her eyes and ears. By the time she reached the common where she had met her husband, she was shivering and weak on her legs. The thought of her lost husband added to her misery at the loss of the

puppies. She had eaten nothing since the previous afternoon—
the farmer gave her only one meal a day. At last, faint with
hunger and utterly broken-spirited, she collapsed. And there,
not long after, Mrs. Dearly found her.

That was Perdita's whole story; except that she never told
Pongo that the farmer had named her Spotty—because she
liked Perdita so much better.

Pongo sympathized with all his heart and did his best to
comfort her. He said he did not think the puppies were lost.
It was more likely that they had been sold—perhaps to the
stranger who came to see them. And this might be the best
thing that could have happened to them—for if they were
valuable, they were sure to be well taken care of. There would
never have been enough food at the farm for them when they
got really big. Perdita knew all this was true. And the two tiny
puppies in the basket with her were wonderfully comforting—
so were the kind things Pongo said about being grateful to her
for feeding them. Soon she felt much happier and slid into a
warm, well-fed sleep.

Pongo lay awake for a long time, wishing Missis and all the
puppies could be with him in the firelit kitchen. He strolled
over and looked at the two puppies asleep with Perdita, and
felt proud and protective—and extremely sorry for Perdita.
Really, she was a very pretty girl—if not a patch on his Missis.

Then he went back to his basket, had a last wash, and settled
down. The fire sank lower; soon the kitchen was lit only by a
faint light from a street lamp on the Outer Circle. Pongo slept.
Perdita slept. And the two puppies, who had come successfully
through their first day in the world, slept as peacefully as if
they had been with their own mother.

Up in the cupboard, Missis had just served supper for eight and was a trifle tired. Mr. Dearly had just served supper for five and was so exhausted by his day of puppy-feeding that he had to crawl out of the cupboard on his hands and knees. Mrs. Dearly got him to bed and fed him with hot milk from a Thermos. They slept with their door open, in case Missis needed anything, but she was very peaceful—though just before she fell asleep she did wonder a little about the strange female down in the kitchen with Pongo. She didn't *worry*, exactly; she just *wondered*.

On the top floor, Nanny Cook slept dreaming of Dalmatian puppies dressed as babies, and Nanny Butler slept dreaming of babies dressed as Dalmatian puppies.

What with four humans, three dogs, and fifteen puppies, it really was a very sleep-full house.

Cruella de Vil
Pays Two Calls

THE next day five more puppies were brought down to Perdita, and she fed them splendidly. So Mr. Dearly went to his business. He hurried back early to do some pup-feeding and found that Mrs. Dearly was feeding the upstairs puppies and the Nannies were taking it in turns to feed the kitchen puppies. He was a little jealous but soon got over it—for he knew that what really mattered was that pups should get plenty of milk without exhausting Missis and poor, thin Perdita too much.

Perdita now had her bed in the dresser cupboard, where there would not be too much light for the puppies' eyes. These began to open in eight days. And a week after that, the puppies' spots began to show.

What a day it was when Mr. Dearly sighted the first spot! After that, spots came thick and fast, though they would not all be through for some months. In a very few days it was possible to recognize every pup by its spots. There were seven girls and eight boys. The prettiest of all the girls was the tiny pup whose life Mr. Dearly had saved at birth, but she was very small and delicate. When pigs have families, the smallest, weakest piglet is often called the cadpig. Mr. Dearly always called the tiny puppy Cadpig, which can be a nice little name when spoken with love.

Patch, the pup born with a black ear, was still the biggest and strongest puppy. He always seemed to be next to Cadpig, as if these two already knew they were going to be special friends. There was a fat, funny boy-puppy called Roly Poly, who was always getting into mischief. And the most striking pup of all was one who had a perfect horseshoe of spots on his back—and had therefore been named Lucky. He was ter- rifically energetic and showed from the beginning that he was going to be the ringleader of all his brothers and sisters.

A few days after the first spots came through, something very upsetting happened: Perdita's milk supply failed. She was miserable about it because she loved the seven pups she had been feeding as much as if they were her own. And she was very, very frightened. Now that she was no longer useful, why should the Dearlys keep her in this warm, comfortable house where—for the first time in her life—she had been given enough to eat? But it was not the food and warmth that mat- tered most to her. It was the love. She had been treated as one of the family. The thought of leaving it all was more than she could bear.

34

And what happened to dogs nobody wanted? All sorts of fears awoke in her heart.

The morning she found she had no milk to offer at all, she crept unhappily out of the dresser cupboard and saw Mrs. Dearly having a mid-morning cup of tea with the Nannies. Mrs. Dearly held out a biscuit. Perdita did not take it. She just laid her head against Mrs. Dearly's knee and gave a little moan.

Mrs. Dearly stoked her and said, "Poor Perdita! I wish we could explain to her that we are helping to feed her seven puppies, so she doesn't need to worry. Darling Perdita, you are *washing* them beautifully and keeping them warm at night. We couldn't possibly do without you."

She had no hope of being understood; she just thought her soothing tone would be comforting. But Perdita was picking up more and more human words every day and understood perfectly. She was wild with relief. For the first time she showed really high spirits, jumping up and kissing Mrs. Dearly, then dashing back to wash the puppies all over again.

Not many days after this, all pups began learning to lap milk for themselves and could soon eat milk puddings and bread soaked in gravy. They were now much too big to go on living in cupboards. Missis and her eight were moved down to the laundry, while Perdita's seven had the run of the kitchen—where they got terribly under the Nannies' feet.

"What a pity they can't be in the laundry with their brothers and sisters," said Nanny Cook one morning.

"Missis might hurt them—she wouldn't know them for her own now," said Nanny Butler. "And she and Perdita would fight."

35

Pongo heard this and decided something must be done. For he knew that, whatever *usual* dogs would do, Missis *would* know her own puppies and she and Perdita would *not* fight. So he had a word with Missis, under the laundry door, and that afternoon, when the Nannies were upstairs, he took a flying leap at the door and managed to burst it open. Out hurtled Missis and eight puppies, and when the Nannies came downstairs they found Pongo, Missis, and Perdita all playing happily with fifteen puppies—who were now so mixed up that it took the Nannies all their time to decide which pups had been brought up by which mother.

After that, all pups lived in the laundry. The door was kept open and a piece of wood was put across it high enough to keep all puppies in—but low enough to be jumped by Missis and Perdita when they wanted to come into the kitchen.

By now it was December, but the days were fine and surprisingly warm, so the puppies were able to play in the area several times a day. They were quite safe there, for the gate at the top of the steps which led to the street now had a strong spring to keep it closed. One morning, when the three dogs and the fifteen puppies were taking the air, Pongo saw a tall woman looking down over the area railings.

He recognized her at once. It was Cruella de Vil.

As usual, she was wearing her absolutely simple white mink cloak, but she now had a brown mink coat under it. Her hat was made of fur, her boots were lined with fur, and she wore big fur gloves.

"What will she wear when it's really cold?" thought Nanny Butler, coming out into the area.

Cruella opened the gate and walked down the steps, saying how pretty the puppies were. Lucky, always the ringleader, came running towards her and nibbled at the fur round the tops of her boots. She picked him up and placed him against her cloak, as if he were something to be worn.

"Such a pretty horseshoe," she said, looking at the spots on his back. "But they all have pretty markings. Are they old enough to leave their mother yet?"

"Very nearly," said Nanny Butler. "But they won't have to. Mr. and Mrs. Dearly are going to keep them *all*." (Sometimes the Nannies wondered just how this was going to be managed.)

"How nice!" said Cruella, and began going up the steps, still holding Lucky against her cloak. Pongo, Missis, and Perdita all barked sharply, and Lucky reached up and nipped Cruella's ear. She gave a scream and dropped him. Nanny Butler was quick enough to catch him in her apron.

"That woman!" said Nanny Cook, who had just come out into the area. "She's enough to frighten the spots off a pup. What's the matter, Lucky?"

For Lucky had dashed into the laundry and was gulping down water. Cruella's ear had tasted of pepper.

Every day now, the puppies grew stronger and more independent. They now fed themselves entirely, eating shredded meat as well as soaked bread and milk puddings. Missis and Perdita were quite happy to leave them now for an hour or more at a time, so the three grown-up dogs took Mrs. Dearly and Nanny Butler for a good walk in the park every morning, while Nanny Cook got the lunch and kept an eye on the puppies. One morning, when she had just let them out into the area, the front doorbell rang.

It was Cruella de Vil, and when she heard Mrs. Dearly was out she said she would come in and wait. She asked many questions about the Dearlys and the puppies and went on talking so long that at last Nanny Cook said she really must go down and let the puppies in, as a cold wind was blowing. Cruella then said she would walk in the park and hope to meet Mrs. Dearly. "Perhaps I can see her from here," she said, strolling to the window.

Nanny Cook also went to the window, intending to point out the nearest way into the park. As she did so, she noticed a small black van standing in front of the house. At that very moment it drove off at a great pace.

Cruella suddenly seemed in a hurry. She almost ran out of the house and down the front-door steps.

"Can't think how she can move so fast, huddled in all those furs," thought Nanny Cook, closing the front door. "And those poor pups, in only their own thin little skins, catching their death of cold."

She hurried down to the kitchen and opened the door to the area.

Not a pup was in sight.

"They're playing me a trick. They're hiding," Nanny Cook told herself. But she knew there was nowhere for fifteen puppies to hide. All the same, she looked behind every tub of shrubs—where not even a mouse could have hidden. The gate at the top of the steps was firmly closed—and no pup could possibly have opened it. Still, she ran up to the street and searched wildly.

"They've been stolen, I know they have!" she moaned,

bursting into tears. "They must have been in that black van I saw driving away."

Cruella de Vil seemed to have changed her mind about going into the park. She was already halfway back to her own house, walking very fast indeed.

Hark, Hark, the Dogs Do Bark!

THROUGH her tears, Nanny Cook stared towards the park. She could now see Mrs. Dearly, Nanny Butler, and the three dogs, who had just turned for home. It seemed a strange and terrible thing that they could be strolling along so happily, when every step brought them nearer to such dreadful news.

As they came across the Outer Circle, Nanny Cook ran to meet them—crying so much that Mrs. Dearly found it hard to understand what had happened. The dogs heard the word "puppies," saw Nanny Cook's tears, and rushed down to the area. Then they went dashing over the whole house, searching, searching. Every few minutes Missis and Perdita howled, and Pongo barked furiously.

While the dogs searched and the Nannies cried on each other's shoulders, Mrs. Dearly telephoned Mr. Dearly. He came home at once, bringing with him one of the Top Men from Scotland Yard. The Top Man found a bit of sacking on the area railings and said the puppies must have been dropped into sacks and driven away in the black van. He promised to Comb the Underworld, but warned the Dearlys that stolen dogs were seldom recovered unless a reward was offered. A reward seemed an unreasonable thing to offer to a thief, but Mr. Dearly was willing to offer it.

He rushed to Fleet Street and had large advertisements put on the front pages of the evening papers (this was rather expensive) and arranged for even larger advertisements to be on the front pages of the next day's morning papers (this was even more expensive). Beyond this, there seemed nothing he or Mrs. Dearly could do except try to comfort each other and comfort the Nannies and the dogs. Soon the Nannies stopped crying and joined in the comforting, and prepared beautiful meals which nobody felt like eating. And at last night fell on the stricken household.

Worn out, the three dogs lay in their baskets in front of the kitchen fire.

"Think of my baby Cadpig in a sack," said Missis with a sob.

"Her big brother Patch will take care of her," said Pongo soothingly—though he felt most unsoothed himself.

"Lucky is so brave, he will bite the thieves," wailed Perdita. "And then they will kill him."

"No, they won't," said Pongo. "The pups were stolen because they are valuable. No one will kill them. They are only valuable while they are alive."

But even as he said this, a terrible suspicion was forming in his mind. And it grew and grew as the night wore on. Long after Missis and Perdita, utterly exhausted, had fallen asleep, he lay awake, staring at the fire, chewing the wicker of his basket as a man might have smoked a pipe.

Anyone who did not know Pongo well would have thought him handsome, amusing, and charming, but not particularly clever. Even the Dearlys did not quite realize the depths of his mind. He was often still so puppyish. He would run after balls and sticks, climb into laps far too small to hold him, roll over on his back to have his stomach scratched. How was anyone to guess that this playful creature owned one of the keenest brains in Dogdom?

It was at work now. All through the long December night he put two and two together and made four. Once or twice he almost made five.

He had no intention of alarming Missis and Perdita with his suspicions. Poor Pongo! He not only suffered on his own account, as a father; he also suffered on the account of two mothers. (For he had come to feel the puppies *had* two mothers, though he never felt he had two wives—he looked on Perdita as a much loved young sister.) He would say nothing about his worst fears until he was quite sure. Meanwhile, there was an important task ahead of him. He was still planning it when the Nannies came down to start another day.

As a rule, this was a splendid time—with the fire freshly made, plenty of food around, and the pupppies at their most playful. This morning—well, as Nanny Butler said, it just didn't bear thinking about. But she thought about it, and so did everybody else in that pupless house.

No good news came during the day, but the Dearlys were surprised and relieved to find that the dogs ate well. (Pongo had been firm: "You girls have got to keep your strength up.") And there was an even greater surprise in the afternoon. Pongo and Missis showed very plainly that they wanted to take the Dearlys for a walk. Perdita did not. She was determined to stay at home in case any pup returned and was in need of a wash.

Cold weather had come at last—Christmas was only a week away.

"Missis must wear her coat," said Mrs. Dearly.

It was a beautiful blue coat with a white binding; Missis was very proud of it. Coats had been bought for Pongo and Perdita too. But Pongo had made it clear he disliked wearing his.

So the coat was put on Missis, and both dogs were dressed in their handsome chain collars. And then they put the Dearlys on their leashes and led them into the park.

From the first it was quite clear the dogs knew just where they wanted to go. Very firmly they led the way right across the park, across the road, and to the open space which is called Primrose Hill. This did not surprise the Dearlys as it had always been a favourite walk. What did surprise them was the way Pongo and Missis behaved when they got to the top of the hill. They stood side by side and they barked.

They barked to the north, they barked to the south, they barked to the east and west. And each time they changed their positions they began the barking with three very strange short, sharp barks.

"Anyone would think they were signalling," said Mr. Dearly.

But he did not really mean it. And they *were* signalling.

Many people must have noticed how dogs like to bark in the early evening. Indeed, twilight has sometimes been called "Dogs' Barking Time." Busy town dogs bark less than country dogs, but all dogs know all about the Twilight Barking. It is their way of keeping in touch with distant friends, passing on important news, enjoying a good gossip. But none of the dogs who answered Pongo and Missis expected to enjoy a gossip, for the three short, sharp barks meant "Help! Help! Help!"

No dog sends that signal unless the need is desperate. And no dog who hears it ever fails to respond.

Within a few minutes the news of the stolen puppies was travelling across England, and every dog who heard at once turned detective. Dogs living in London's Underworld (hard-bitten characters, also hard-biting) set out to explore sinister alleys where dog thieves lurk. Dogs in Pet Shops hastened to make quite sure all puppies offered for sale were not Dalmatians in disguise. And dogs who could do nothing else swiftly handed on the news, spreading it through London and on through the suburbs, and on, on to the open country: "Help! Help! Help! Fifteen Dalmatian puppies stolen. Send news to Pongo and Missis Pongo, of Regent's Park, London. End of message."

Pongo and Missis hoped all this would be happening. But all they really knew was that they had made contact with the dogs near enough to answer them, and that those dogs would be standing by, at twilight the next evening, to relay any news that had come along.

45

One Great Dane, over towards Hampstead, was particularly encouraging.

"I have a chain of friends all over England," he said in his great, booming bark. "And I will be on duty day and night. Courage, courage, O Dogs of Regent's Park!"

It was almost dark now. And the Dearlys were suggesting— very gently—that they should be taken home. So after a few last words with the Great Dane, Pongo and Missis led the way down Primrose Hill. The dogs who had answered them were silent now, but the Twilight Barking was spreading in an ever-widening circle. And tonight it would not end with twilight. It would go on and on as the moon rose high over England.

The next day a great many people who had read Mr. Dearly's advertisements rang up to sympathize. (Cruella de Vil did, and seemed most upset when she was told the puppies had been stolen while she was talking to Nanny Cook.) But no one had anything helpful to say. And Scotland Yard was Frankly Baffled. So it was another sad, sad day for the Dearlys, the Nannies, and the dogs.

Just before dusk, Pongo and Missis again showed that they wished to take the Dearlys for a walk. So off they started, and again the dogs led the way to the top of Primrose Hill. And again they stood side by side and gave three sharp barks. But this time, though no human ear could have detected it, they were slightly different barks. And they meant, not "Help! Help! Help!" but "Ready! Ready! Ready!"

The dogs who had collected news from all over London replied first. Reports had come in from the West End and the East End and south of the Thames. And all these reports were the same.

46

"Calling Pongo and Missis Pongo of Regent's Park. No news of your puppies. Deepest regrets. End of message."

Poor Missis! She had hoped so much that her pups were still in London. Pongo's secret suspicion had led him to pin his hopes to news from the country. And soon it was pouring in—some of it relayed across London. But it was always the same.

"Calling Pongo and Missis Pongo of Regent's Park. No news of your puppies. Deepest regrets. End of message."

Again and again Pongo and Missis barked the "Ready!" signal, each time with fresh hope. Again and again came bitter disapointment. At last only the Great Dane over towards Hampstead remained to be heard from. They signalled to him—their last hope!

Back came his booming bark.

"Calling Pongo and Missis Pongo of Regent's Park. No news of your puppies. Deepest regrets. End of—"

The Great Dane stopped in mid-bark. A second later he barked again. "Wait! Wait Wait!"

Dead still, their hearts thumping, Pongo and Missis waited. They waited so long that Mr. Dearly put his hand on Pongo's head and said, "What about coming home, boy?" For the first time in his life, Pongo jerked his head from Mr. Dearly's hand, then went on standing stock still. And at last the Great Dane spoke again, booming triumphantly through the fast gathering dusk.

"Calling Pongo and Missis Pongo. News! News at last! Stand by to receive details."

A most wonderful thing had happened. Just as the Great Dane had been about to sign off, a Pomeranian with a piercing

47

yap had got a message through to him. She had heard it from a Poodle who had heard it from a Boxer who had heard it from a Pekinese. Dogs of almost every known breed had helped to carry the news—and a great many dogs of unknown breed (none the worse for that, and all of them bright as buttons). In all, four hundred and eighty dogs had relayed the message, which had travelled over sixty miles as the dog barks. Each dog had given the "Urgent" signal, which had silenced all gossiping dogs. Not that many dogs were merely gossiping that night; almost all the Twilight Barking had been about the missing puppies.

This was the strange story that now came through to Pongo and Missis: Some hours earlier, an elderly English Sheepdog, living on a farm in a remote Suffolk village, had gone for an afternoon amble. He knew all about the missing puppies and had just been discussing them with the tabby cat at the farm. She was a great friend of his.

Some little way from the village, on a lonely heath, was an old house completely surrounded by an unusually high wall. Two brothers, named Saul and Jasper Baddun lived there, but were merely caretakers for the real owner. The place had an evil reputation—no local dog would have dreamed of putting its nose inside the tall iron gates. In any case, these gates were always kept locked.

It so happened that the Sheepdog's walk took him past this house. He quickened his pace, having no wish to meet either of the Badduns. And at that moment, something came sailing out over the high wall.

It was a bone, the Sheepdog saw with pleasure; but not a bone with meat on it, he noted with disgust. It was an old, dry bone, and on it were some peculiar scratches. The scratches formed letters. And the letters were S.O.S.

Someone was asking for help! Someone behind the tall wall and the high, chained gates! The Sheepdog barked a low, cautious bark. He was answered by a high, shrill bark. Then he heard a yelp, as if some dog had been cuffed. The Sheepdog barked again, saying, "I'll do all I can." Then he picked up the bone in his teeth and raced back to the farm.

Once home, he showed the bone to the tabby cat and asked her help. Then, together, they hurried to the lonely house. At the back they found a tree whose branches reached over the wall. The cat climbed the tree, went along its branches, and then leaped to a tree the other side of the wall.

"Take care of yourself," barked the Sheepdog. "Remember those Baddun brothers are villains."

The cat clawed her way down, backwards, to the ground, then hurried through the overgrown shrubbery. Soon she came to an old brick wall which enclosed a stableyard. From behind the wall came whimperings and snufflings. She leaped to the top of the wall and looked down.

The next second, one of the Baddun brothers saw her and threw a stone at her. She dodged it, jumped from the wall, and ran for her life. In two minutes she was safely back with the Sheepdog.

"They're there!" she said triumphantly. "The place is *seething* with Dalmatian puppies!"

The Sheepdog was a formidable Twilight Barker. Tonight, with the most important news in Dogdom to send out, he surpassed himself. And so the message travelled, by way of farm dogs and house dogs, great dogs and small dogs. Sometimes a bark would carry half a mile or more; sometimes it would need to carry only a few yards. One sharp-eared Cairn saved the chain from breaking by picking up a bark from nearly a mile away and then almost bursting herself getting it on to the dog next door. Across miles and miles of country, across miles and miles of suburbs, across a network of London streets, the chain held firm; from the depths of Suffolk to the top of Primrose Hill—where Pongo and Missis, still as statues, stood listening, listening.

"Puppies found in lonely house. S.O.S. on old bone . . ." Missis could not take it all in. But Pongo missed nothing. There were instructions for reaching the village, suggestions for the journey, offers of hospitality on the way. And the dog chain was standing by to take a message back to the pups— the Sheepdog would bark it over the wall in the dead of night.

At first Missis was too excited to think of anything to say, but Pongo barked clearly, "Tell them we're coming! Tell them we start tonight! Tell them to be brave!"

Then Missis found her voice. "Give them all our love! Tell Patch to take care of the Cadpig! Tell Lucky not to be too daring! Tell Roly Poly to keep out of mischief!" She would have sent a message to every one of the fifteen pups if Pongo had not whispered, "That's enough, dear. We mustn't make it too complicated. Let the Great Dane start work now."

So they signed off and there was a sudden silence. And then, though not quite so loudly, they heard the Great Dane again. But this time he was not barking towards them. What they heard was their message, starting on its way to Suffolk.

To the Rescue!

As they walked the Dearlys home, Pongo said to Missis, "Did you hear who owns the house where the puppies are imprisoned?"

Missis said, "No, Pongo, I'm afraid I missed many things the Great Dane barked."

"I will tell you everything later," said Pongo.

He was faced with a problem. He now knew that his terrible suspicions were justified and it was time Missis learned the truth. But if he told her before dinner, she might lose her appetite, and if he told her afterwards, she might lose her dinner. So still he said nothing. And he made her eat every crumb of dinner and then join him in asking for more—which the Nannies gave with delight.

51

"It may be a long time before we get another meal," he explained.

While the Nannies fed the Dearlys, the dogs made their plans. Perdita at once offered to come to Suffolk with them.

"But you are still much too delicate for the journey, dear Perdita," said Missis. "Besides, what could you do?"

"I could *wash* the puppies," said Perdita.

Both Pongo and Missis then said they knew Perdita was a beautiful puppy-washer but her job must be to comfort the Dearlys. And she felt that herself.

"If only we could make them understand why we are leaving them!" said Missis, sadly.

"If we could do that, we shouldn't have to leave them," said Pongo. "They would drive us to Suffolk in the car. And send the police."

"Oh, let us have one more try to speak their language," said Missis.

The Dearlys were sitting by the fire in the big white drawing room. They welcomed the two dogs and offered them the sofa. But Pongo and Missis had no wish for a comfortable nap. They stood together, looking imploringly at the Dearlys.

Then Pongo barked gently, "Wuff, wuff, *wuffolk!*"

Mr. Dearly patted him but understood nothing.

Then Missis tried. "Wuff, wuff, *wuffolk!*"

"Are you telling us the puppies are in Suffolk?" said Mrs. Dearly.

The dogs wagged their tails wildly. Buy Mrs. Dearly was only joking. It was hopeless, and the dogs knew it always would be.

52

Dogs can never speak the language of humans, and humans can never speak the language of dogs. But many dogs can understand almost every word humans say, while humans seldom learn to recognize more than half a dozen barks, if that. And barks are only a small part of the dog language. A wagging tail can mean so many things. Humans know that it means a dog is pleased, but not what a dog is saying about his pleasedness. (Really, it is very clever of humans to understand a wagging tail at all, as they have no tails of their own.) Then there are the snufflings and sniffings, the pricking of ears—all meaning different things. And many, many words are expressed by a dog's eyes.

It was with their eyes that Pongo and Missis spoke most that evening, for they knew the Dearlys could at least understand one eye-word. That word was "love," and the dogs said it again and again, leaning their heads against the Dearlys' knees. And the Dearlys said, "Dear Pongo," "Dear Missis," again and again.

"They're asking us to find their puppies, I know they are," said Mrs. Dearly, never guessing that, as well as declaring their love, the dogs were saying, "We are going to find the puppies. Please forgive us for leaving you. Please have faith in our safe return."

At eleven o'clock the dogs gave Mrs. Dearly's hand one last kiss and took Mr. Dearly out for his last run. Perdita joined them for this. She had spent the evening with the Nannies, feeling that Pongo and Missis might wish to be alone with their pets. Then all three dogs went to their baskets in the warm kitchen and the house settled for the night.

But it did not settle for long. Shortly before midnight Pongo

53

and Missis got up, ate some biscuits they had hidden, and took long drinks of water. Then they said a loving good-bye to Perdita, who was in tears, nosed open a window at the back of the house, and got out into the mews. (They knew they could not open the gate at the top of the area steps.) Carefully they nosed the window shut, so that Perdita would not get a chill, and then went round to the area railings to give her one last smile. (Dogs smile in various ways: Pongo and Missis smiled by wrinkling their noses.) She was there at the kitchen window, bravely trying to wag her tail.

Beyond Perdita, Missis could see the three cushioned baskets in the rosy glow from the fire. She thought of the many peaceful nights she had spent in hers, in the happy days when a dog could fall asleep looking forward to breakfast. Poor Missis! Of course she loved Pongo, the puppies, the Dearlys, and the Nannies—and dear, kind Perdita—best of everything in the world. But she also loved her creature comforts. Never had her home seemed so dear to her as now when she was leaving it for a dangerous, unknown world.

And it was such a cold world. The night was fine, the stars were brilliant, but the wind was keen. If only she could have brought her beautiful blue coat, now hanging on a peg in the warm kitchen!

Pongo saw her shiver. It is a hard thing for a loving husband to see his wife shiver.

"Are you cold, Missis?" he asked anxiously.

"No, Pongo," said Missis, still shivering.

"*I* am," said Pongo untruthfully. "But I shall soon warm up."

He tail-wagged good-bye to Perdita, then started off briskly

54

along the Outer Circle, looking very spirited. Missis kept pace with him; but after its last wag to Perdita, her tail went down.

After a few minutes, Pongo said, "Are you warmer now, Missis?"

"Yes, Pongo," said Missis, still shivering. And still her tail was down.

Pongo knew that if he could not cheer her up she would never be able to face the hardships that lay ahead. And he thought he could do with some cheering up himself. So he began a little speech, intended to give them both courage.

"I sometimes think," he said, "that you and I have become a bit pampered. Well, pampering does good dogs no harm, provided they don't come to depend on it. If they do, they become old before their time. We should never lose our liking for adventure, never forget our wild ancestry." (They were then passing the Zoo.) "Oh, I know we are worried about the puppies, but the more we worry, the less we shall be able to help them. We must be brave, we must even be gay, we must know we *cannot* fail. Are you warmer now, Missis?"

"Yes, Pongo," said Missis. But still she shivered and still her tail drooped.

They were now nearly at the bridge which leads from the Outer Circle towards Camden Town.

"Stop for a moment," said Pongo. And he turned and looked back along the curve of the Circle. No car was in sight, no light was in any window. The lamp-posts were like sentinels guarding the sleeping park.

"Think of the day when we come back with fifteen puppies running behind us," said Pongo.

"Oh, Pongo, are you *sure?*"

55

"Absolutely sure," said Pongo. "Are you a little warmer now, dear Missis?"

"Yes, Pongo," said Missis, "And this time it is true."

"Then onwards to Suffolk!" said Pongo.

And as they ran towards the bridge, Missis carried her tail as high as his.

"Not *too* high, Missis dear," said Pongo. "Let our hearts be gay, but not our tails." For when a Dalmatian's tail is curled high over the back it is called a "gay" tail and is a bad fault.

Missis was still laughing at this little joke when her heart gave a wild flutter. Coming towards them was a policeman.

Instantly Pongo led the way into a back street, and they were soon safely out of the policeman's sight. But seeing him had reminded Missis of something.

"Oh, Pongo!" she wailed. "We are *illegal*. We are out without our collars."

"And a good thing, too," said Pongo, "for a dog can be grabbed by the collar. But I do wish we could have brought your coat." He had noticed that she was shivering again—though this time it was because she had been scared by the policeman.

"*I* don't," said Missis bravely. "For if I wore a coat, how should I know how cold the puppies were? They have no coats. Oh, Pongo, how can they make the journey from Suffolk in such wintry weather? Suppose it snows?"

"They may not have to make the journey *yet*," said Pongo.

Missis stared in astonishment. "But we must get them back quickly or the dog thieves will sell them."

"Nothing will happen to them *yet*," said Pongo. And now

56

he knew it was time to tell his wife the truth. "Let's rest a moment," he said, and led Missis into the shelter of a doorway. Then he went on gently.

"Dear Missis, our puppies were not stolen by ordinary dog thieves. Try not to be too frightened. Remember we are going to rescue them. Our puppies were stolen by Cruella de Vil's orders—so that she can have their skins made into a fur coat. Oh, Missis, be brave!"

Missis had collapsed. She lay on the doorstep, panting, her eyes full of horror.

"But it will be *all right*, dear Missis! They will be safe for months yet. They are much too small to be—to be used for a fur coat yet."

Missis shuddered. Then she struggled to her feet.

"I will go back!" she cried. "I will go back and tear Cruella De Vil to pieces."

"That would do no good at all," said Pongo firmly. "We must rescue the puppies first and think of our revenge later. On to Suffolk!"

"On to Suffolk, then!" said Missis, staggering along on shaky legs. "But we shall come back, Cruella de Vil!"

Soon Missis began to feel better, for Pongo made her see that puppies whose skins were wanted for a fur coat would be well fed and well taken care of, and kept together. Ordinary dog thieves might have sold them already, and to different people. She asked him many questions, and he told of his early suspicions—how he had suddenly recalled the evening they had first seen Cruella and sat under the piano in the red drawing room.

"She said we would make enchanting fur coats, Missis."

"For spring wear, over a black suit," said Missis, remembering. "And she did take a lot of interest in the puppies."

"And she kept Nanny Cook talking while they were stolen," said Pongo. "But I wasn't *quite* sure until this evening, at the Twilight Barking. You didn't hear as much as I did, Missis. Our puppies are at Hell Hall, the ancestral home of the de Vils."

And he knew, though he kept this from Missis, that the S.O.S. on the old bone meant "Save Our Skins."

At the Old Inn

Pongo had no difficulty in taking the right road out of London, for he and Mr. Dearly had done much motoring in their bachelor days and often driven to Suffolk. Mile after mile the two dogs ran through the deserted streets, as the December night grew colder. At last London was left behind and, just before dawn, they reached a village in Epping Forest where they hoped to spend the day.

They had decided they must always travel by night and rest during daylight. For they felt sure Mr. Dearly would advertise their loss and the police would be on the lookout for them. There was far less chance of their being seen and caught by night.

They had barely entered the sleeping village when they heard a quiet bark. The next moment a burly Golden Retriever was greeting them.

"Pongo and Missis Pongo, I presume? All arrangements were made for you by Late Twilight Barking. Please follow me."

He led them to an old gabled inn and then under an archway to a cobbled yard.

"Please drink here, at my own bowl," he said. "Food awaits you in your sleeping quarters, but water could not be arranged."

(For no dog can carry a full water-bowl.)

Pongo and Missis had had only one drink since they left home, at an old drinking trough for horses, which had a lower trough for dogs. They now gulped thirstily and gratefully.

"My pride as an innkeeper tempts me to offer you one of our best bedrooms," said the Golden Retriever. "They combine old-world charm with all modern conveniences—and no charge for breakfast in bed. But it wouldn't be wise."

"No, indeed," said Pongo. "We might be discovered."

"Exactly. We are putting you in the safest place any of us could think of. Naturally every dog in the village came to the meeting after the Late Barking—when we heard this village was to have the honour of receiving you. Step this way."

At the far end of the yard were some old stables, and in the last stable of all was a broken-down stagecoach.

"Just the right place for Dalmatians," said Pongo, smiling, "for our ancestors were trained to run behind coaches and carriages. Some people still call us Coach Dogs or Carriage Dogs."

60

And your run from London has shown you are worthy of your ancestors," said the Golden Retriever. "When I was a pup we sometimes took this old coach out for the school picnic, but no one has bothered with it for years now. You should be quite safe, and some dogs will always be on guard. In case of sudden alarm, you can go out by the back door of the stable and escape across the fields."

There was a deep bed of straw on the floor of the coach, and neatly laid out on the seat were two magnificent chops, half a dozen iced cakes, and a box of peppermint creams.

"From the butcher's dog, the baker's dog, and the dog at the sweet-shop," said the Retriever. "I shall arrange your dinner. Will steak be satisfactory?"

Pongo and Missis said it would indeed, and tried to thank him for everything, but he waved their thanks away, saying, "It's a very great honour. We are planning a small plaque—to be concealed from human eyes, of course—*saying:* PONGO AND MISSIS SLEPT HERE."

Then he took them to the cobwebbed window and pointed out a smaller edition of himself, who was patrolling the inn courtyard.

My youngest lad, already on guard. He's hoping to see you for a moment, when you're rested, and ask for your pawmarks—to start his collection. A small guard of honour will see you out of the village, but I shan't let them waste too much of your time. Good night—though it's really good morning. Pleasant dreams."

As soon as he had gone, Pongo and Missis ate ravenously.

"Though perhaps we should not eat *too* heavily before going to sleep," said Pongo, so they left a couple of peppermint creams. (Missis later ate them in her sleep.) Then they settled down in the straw, close together, and got warmer and warmer.

Missis said, Do you feel *sure* our puppies will be well fed and well taken care of?"

"*Quite* sure. And they will be safe for a long time, because their spots are nowhere near big enough for a striking fur coat yet. Oh, Missis, how pleasant it is to be on our own like this!"

Missis thumped her tail with joy—and with relief. For there had been moments when she had felt—not jealous, exactly, but just a bit *wistful* about Pongo's affection for Perdita. She loved Perdita, was grateful to her and sorry for her; still—well, it was nice to have her own husband to herself, thought Missis. But she made herself say, "Poor Perdita! No husband, no puppies! We must never let her feel we want to be on our own."

"I do hope she can comfort the Dearlys," said Pongo.

"She will *wash* them," said Missis—and fell asleep.

How gloriously they slept! It was their first really deep sleep since the loss of the puppies. Even the Twilight Barking did not disturb them. It brought good news, which the Retriever told them when he woke them, as soon as it was dark. All was well with the pups, and Lucky sent a message that they were getting more food than they could eat. This gave Pongo and Missis a wonderful appetite for the steaks that were waiting for them.

While they ate, they chatted to the Retriever and his wife and their family, who lived at various houses in the village. And the Retriever told Pongo how to reach the village where the next day was to be spent—this had been arranged by the Twilight Barking. The steaks were finished and a nice piece of cheese was going down well when the Corgi from the post office arrived with an evening paper in her mouth. Mr. Dearly had put in his largest advertisement yet—with a photograph of Pongo and Missis (taken during the joint honeymoon).

Pongo's heart sank, for he felt the route planned for them was no longer safe. It led through many villages, where even by night they might be noticed—unless they waited till all humans had gone to bed, which would waste too much time. He said, "We must travel across country."

But you'll get lost," said the Retriever's wife.

"Pongo never loses his way," said Missis proudly.

"And the moon will be nearly full," said the Retriever. "You should manage. But it will be hard to pick up food. I had arranged for it to await you in several villages."

Pongo said they had eaten so much that they could do without food until the morning, but he hated to think dogs might be waiting up for them during the night.

"I will cancel it by the Nine-o'clock Barking," said the Retriever.

There was a snuffling at the back door of the stable. All the dogs of the village had arrived to see Pongo and Missis off.

"We should start at once," said Pongo. "Where's our young friend who wants paw-marks?"

The Retriever's youngest lad stepped forward shyly, carrying an old menu. Pongo and Missis put their pawtographs on the back of it for him, then thanked the Retriever and his family for all they had done.

Outside, two rows of dogs were waiting to cheer. But no human ear could have heared the cheers, for every dog had now seen the photograph in the evening paper and knew an

63

escape must be made in absolute silence.

Pongo and Missis bowed right and left, gratefully sniffing their thanks to all. Then, after a last good-bye to the Retriever, they were off across the moonlit fields.

"On to Suffolk!" said Pongo.

Cross Country

THEY were well rested and well fed, and they soon reached a pond where they could drink—the Retriever had told them to be on the lookout for it. (It would not have been safe for them to drink from his bowl again; too many humans were now about.) And their spirits were far higher than when they had left the house in Regent's Park. How far away it already seemed, although it was less than twenty-four hours since they had been in their baskets by the kitchen fire. Of course they were still anxious about their puppies, and sorry for the poor Dearlys. But Lucky's message had been cheering, and they hoped to make it all up to the Dearlys one day. And anyway, as Pongo said, worrying would help nobody, while enjoying their freedom to race across the fields would do them a power of good.

He was relieved to see how well Missis ran and what good condition she was in. So much food had been given to her while she was feeding the puppies that she had never got pitifully thin—as Perdita had when she had fed her own puppies without being given extra food.

"You are a beautiful dog, Missis," said Pongo. "I am very proud of you."

At this, Missis looked even more beautiful and Pongo felt even prouder of her. After a minute or so, he said, "Do you think *I'm* looking pretty fit?"

Missis told him he looked magnificent, and wished she had said so without being asked. He was not a vain dog, but every husband likes to know that his wife admires him.

They ran on, shoulder to shoulder, a perfectly matched couple. The night was windless and therefore seemed warmer than the night before, but Pongo knew there was a heavy frost; and when, after a couple of hours across the fields, they came to another pond, there was a film of ice over it. They broke this easily and drank, but Pongo began to be a little anxious about where they would be by daybreak, for they would need good shelter in such cold weather. As they were now travelling across country, he thought it unlikely they would find the village that had been expecting them, but he felt sure most dogs would by now have heard of them and would be willing to help. "Only we must be near some village by dawn, or we shall meet no dogs," he thought.

Soon after that a lane crossed the fields and, as they had just heard a church clock strike midnight, Pongo felt there

was now little chance of their meeting any humans on the road. He wanted to find a signpost and make sure they were travelling in the right direction. So they went along the lane for a mile until they came to a sleeping village. There was a signpost on the green, which Pongo read by the light of the moon. (He was very good at reading—as a pup he had played with alphabet blocks.) All was well. Their journey across the fields had saved them many miles, and they were now deep in Essex. (The village where they might have stayed was already behind them.) By going north, they would reach Suffolk.

The only depressing thing was that the wonderful steak dinner seemed such a long time ago, And there was no hope of getting food as late as this. They just had to go on and on through the night, getting hungrier and hungrier.

And by the time it began to get light, they were also extremely chilly—partly because they were hungry and tired and partly because it was getting colder and colder. The ice on the ponds they passed was thicker and thicker—at last they came to a pond where they could not break through to drink.

And now Pongo was really anxious, for they had reached a part of the country where there seemed to be very few villages. Where could they get food and shelter? Where could they hide and sleep during the bitterly cold day ahead of them?

He did not tell Missis of his fears and she would not even admit that she was hungry. But her tail drooped and her pace got slower and slower. He felt terrible: tired, hungry, anxious, and deeply ashamed that he was letting his beautiful wife suffer hardship. Surely there would be a village soon, or a fair-sized farm?

"Should we rest a little now, Pongo?" said Missis at last.

68

"Not until we've found some dogs to help us, Missis," said Pongo. Then his heart gave a glad leap. Ahead of them were some thatched cottages! It was full daylight now, and he could see smoke twisting up from several chimneys. Surely some dog would be about.

If anyone tries to catch us, we must take to the fields and run," said Pongo.

"Yes, Pongo," said Missis, though she did not now feel she could run very far.

They reached the first cottage. Pongo gave a low bark. No dog answered it.

They went on and soon saw that this was not a real village but just a short row of cottages, some of them empty and almost in ruins. Except for smoke rising from a few chimneys, there was no sign of life until they came to the very last cottage. As they reached it a little boy looked out of a window.

He saw them and quickly opened the cottage door. In his hand was a thick slab of bread and butter. He appeared to be holding it out to them.

"Gently, Pongo," said Missis, "or we shall frighten him."

They went through the open gate and up the cobbled path, wagging their tails and looking with love at the little boy— and the bread and butter. The child smiled at them fearlessly and waved the bread and butter. And then, when they were only three or four yards away, he stooped, picked up a stone, and slung it with all his force. He gave a squeal of laughter when he saw the stone strike Pongo, then went in and slammed the door.

At that moment the dogs heard a man's voice inside the

69

cottage. They turned and ran as fast as they could, along the road and then into a field.

"Are you hurt, Pongo?" cried Missis as they ran. Then she saw that he was limping. They stopped behind a haystack. Pongo's leg was bleeding—the stone must have had a very sharp edge. But what hurt him most was the bruise on the bone. He was trembling with pain and rage.

Missis was terrified, but she did not let him see this. She licked his wound and said there was nothing a good rest would not cure.

"Rest? Where?" said Pongo.

Missis saw that the haystack was very loosely made. She scrabbled at it fiercely, saying, "Look, Pongo, you can creep in and get warm. Then sleep for a while. I will find us some food—I will, I will! The first dog I meet will help me."

By now she had made a large hole in the haystack. Pongo looked at it longingly. But no! He could not let her go alone. He struggled to his feet, wincing with pain, and said, "I must come with you to find food. And I will bite that child."

"No, Pongo, no!" cried Missis, horrified. "Remember he is only a very *young* human. All very young creatures are ignorantly cruel—often our dear puppies hurt me badly, not knowing they were doing so. To bite a human is the greatest crime a dog can commit. You shall not let that cruel, thoughtless child put such a sin on your conscience. Your pain and anger will pass, but the guilt would remain with you for always."

Pongo knew she was right, and already the desire to bite the child was passing. "But I won't let you go alone," he said.

"Then let us *both* rest a while first," said crafty Missis. "Come on, there's room for two." And she crept into the haystack.

"We should find food first, or we shall be too weak to find it when we wake up," said Pongo. But he followed her into the haystack.

"Just sleep for a few minutes, Pongo—while I keep guard," said Missis coaxingly.

Pongo could fight on no longer. Sleep came to him while he thought he was still arguing.

Missis waited a few minutes, then crept out and pulled hay round Pongo to hide him. She no longer felt sleepy; she was far too anxious. Even her appetite had gone for the moment. Still, she knew she must find food for them both—and she had no idea how to, for she was almost sure there was no dog anywhere near to help her. But pretending to Pongo that she felt brave had made her really feel a little braver, and her tail was no longer down.

She could still see the thatched cottages, and she noticed some hens at the back of them. Perhaps the hens would have some stale crusts that she could—well, borrow. She went back.

The first cottage she reached was the one where the little boy lived. And now he was at the back, staring at her! This time, he had an even larger slab of bread and butter, with some jam on it. He ran towards her, holding it out.

"Perhaps he really means it now," thought Missis. "Perhaps he's sorry he hurt Pongo." And she went forward hopefully— though well prepared to dodge stones.

The child waited until she was quite close. Then again he

71

stooped for a stone. But he was on a patch of grass, with no stones handy. So, instead, he threw the slab of bread and butter. He threw it with rage, not love, but that made it no less valuable. Missis caught it neatly and bolted.

"Bless me," she thought, "he's just a small human who likes throwing things. His parents should buy him a ball."

She took the bread and butter back to the haystack and laid it down by her sleeping husband's nose. So far she had not even licked it, but now she let herself nibble off one very small corner. It tasted so glorious that her appetite came back with a rush, but she left all the rest for Pongo to find when he woke. Again she pulled the hay round him, and then ran to the road. But she saw a man outside the cottage where the little boy lived, so she did not dare to go back to visit the hens. She ran in the opposite direction.

It was now a very beautiful winter morning. Every blade of grass was silvered with hoarfrost and glittering in the newly risen sun. But Missis was far too worried to enjoy the beauty. The triumph of getting the bread was wearing off, and all sorts of fears were rushing at her.

Suppose Pongo was seriously injured? Suppose he was too lame to go on? Suppose she could find no food close at hand? If she had to go far, she knew she would get lost. She even got lost in Regent's Park, almost every time the Dearlys were off the leash. They often laughed at the way she would stand still, wildly staring round for them. Suppose she never found her way back to Pongo and he searched and searched and never found her? Lost dog! The very words were terrible!

And was she even now quite sure of her way back to the haystack?

"It isn't fair," thought Missis. "No one as worried as I am ought to feel hungry too." For she was ravenous—*and* thirsty. She tried licking the ice in a ditch, but it hurt her tongue without quenching her thirst.

She was beginning to think she must go back and make sure where the haystack was, when she came to an old red-brick archway leading to a long gravel drive. Her spirits rose. Surely this must be the entrance to some big country house, such as she had stayed at several times when she and Mrs. Dearly were both bachelors. Such houses had many dogs, large kitchens, plenty of food. Joyfully she ran through the archway.

She could see no house ahead of her because the drive twisted. It was overgrown with weeds, and it went on so long that she began to wonder if it really did lead to a house. Indeed, it was now so wild and neglected that it seemed more like a path through a wood than the approach to a house. And it was so strangely silent; never in her life had Missis felt quite so alone.

More and more frightened, she ran round one more bend—and suddenly she was out in the open, with the house in front of her.

It was very old, built of mellow red brick, like the archway, with many little diamond-paned windows and one great window that reached almost to the roof. The windows twinkling in the early morning sunshine looked cheerful and welcoming, but there was no sign of life anywhere. And there was grass growing in the cracks of the wide stone steps which led to the massive oak door.

"It's empty!" thought Missis in despair.

But it was *not* empty. Looking out of an open window was a Spaniel, black except for his muzzle, which was grey with age.

"Good morning," he said most courteously. "Can I be of any help to you, my dear?"

Hot Buttered Toast

IT was wonderful how quickly the Spaniel took in the story Missis poured out to him, for he had not heard any news by way of the Twilight Barking.

"Haven't listened to it for years," he said. "Indeed, I doubt if I could get it now. There isn't another dog for miles. Anyway, Sir Charles needs me at twilight—he needs me almost all the time. I'm only off duty now because he's in his bath."

They were now in a large stone-floored kitchen, where the Spaniel had led Missis after inviting her to jump in through the window. He went on. "Breakfast before you tell me any more, young lady," and led her to a large plate of meat.

"But it's *your* breakfast," said Missis, trying not to look as hungry as she felt.

"No, it isn't. It's my supper, if you really want to know. I'd no appetite—and I shan't have any for breakfast, which will be served to me any minute. Tea's my meal. Hurry up, my dear. It will be thrown away if you don't eat it."

Missis took one delicious gulp. Then she stopped. "My husband—"

The Spaniel interrupted her. "We'll see about *his* breakfast later, Finish it all, my child."

So Missis ate and ate and then had a long drink from a white pottery bowl. She had never seen a bowl like it.

"That's an eighteenth century dog's drinking bowl," said the Spaniel, "handed down from dog to dog in this family. And now, before you get too sleepy, you'd better bring your husband here."

"Oh, yes" said Missis eagerly. "Please tell me how to get back to the haystack."

"Just go to the end of the drive and turn left."

"I'm not very good at right and left," said Missis, "especially left."

The Spaniel smiled, then looked at her paws. "This will help you," he said. "That paw with the pretty spot—that is your *right* paw."

"Then which is my left paw?"

"Why, the other paw, of course."

"Back or front?" asked Missis.

"Just forget your back paws."

Missis was puzzled. *Could* she forget her back paws? And if she could, would it be safe?

76

The Spaniel went on. "Look at your front paws and re-member: Right paw, spot. Left paw, no spot."

Missis stared hard at her paws. "I will *practise*," she said earnestly. "But please tell me how to *turn* left."

"Turn on the side of the paw which does not have a spot."

"Whichever way I am going?"

"Certainly," said the Spaniel. "The paw with the spot will always be your right paw. You can depend on that."

"If I turned towards you now, would I be turning left?" asked Missis, after thinking very hard.

"Yes, yes. Splendid!" said the Spaniel.

Missis then turned round and faced the other way. "But now you are on the side of the paw with the spot," she said worriedly, "so my right paw has turned into my left."

The Spaniel gave it up. "I will *show* you the haystack," he said, and led her out through what once must have been a fine kitchen-garden but was now a mass of weeds. Beyond it were the fields. Missis could just see the thatched cottages and the haystack.

"It's the *only* haystack," said the Spaniel. "All the same, keep your eyes on it all the time you run. I would come with you, but my rheumatism prevents me—and Sir Charles will need me to carry his spectacle-case downstairs. We are an old, old couple, my dear. He is ninety, and I—according to a foolish human reckoning that one year of a dog's life represents seven years of human life—I am a hundred and five."

"I should never have guessed it," said Missis politely—and truthfully.

"Anyway, I'm still young enough to know a pretty dog when

77

I see one," said the Spaniel gallantly. "Now off you go for your husband. You'll have no difficulty in finding your way back because you will see our chimneys from the haystack."

"Right or left?" asked Missis brightly.

"In front of your delightful nose. If I'm not here, just take your husband into the kitchen and I'll join you as soon as I can."

Missis raced off happily across the frosty fields, never taking her eyes off the haystack and feeling very proud when she reached it without getting lost. Pongo was still heavily asleep, with the bread and butter by his nose.

Poor Pongo! Waking up was awful, what with his sleepiness, the pain in his leg, and his horror at learning Missis had been dashing about the countryside alone. But he felt better when she had told him the news, which she did while he ate the bread and butter. And though his leg hurt, he found he could run without limping.

"Which way do we go?" he asked as they came out of the haystack.

Missis looked worried. There were no chimneys ahead of her nose—because she was facing in exactly the opposite direction. But Pongo saw the chimneys and took her towards them. Just before they reached the kitchen-garden, Missis said, "Pongo, do dogs have spots on their right paws or on their left paws?"

"That depends on the dog," said Pongo.

Missis shook her head. "It's hopeless," she thought. "How can I depend on a thing that depends?"

The Spaniel was waiting for them.

"I've settled Sir Charles by the fire," he said, "so I've an hour or so to spare. Come to breakfast, my dear fellow."

He led Pongo to the kitchen, where there was now another plate of food.

"Surely it's *your* breakfast, sir," said Pongo.

"Had mine with Sir Charles. Don't as a rule take breakfast, but meeting your pretty wife gave me an appetite, so I accepted a couple of slices of bacon. Sir Charles was *so* pleased. Go ahead, my dear chap, I couldn't eat another bite."

So Pongo ate and ate and drank and drank.

"And now for a long sleep," said the Spaniel.

He led them up a back staircase and along many passages till they came to a large sunny bedroom in which was a four-poster bed. Beside it was a round basket. "Mine," said the Spaniel, "but I never use it. Sir Charles likes me on the bed. Luckily that's made already because John—he's our valet—is already off for his day out. Jump up, both of you."

Pongo and Missis jumped onto the four-poster and relaxed in bliss.

"No one will come up here until this evening," said the Spaniel, "because Sir Charles can't manage the stairs until John gets back. The fire should last some hours yet—we always light it for Sir Charles to have his bath in front of it. No new-fangled plumbing in this house. Sleep well, my children."

The sunlight, the firelight, the tapestried walls were all so beautiful that it seemed a waste not to stay awake and enjoy them. So they did—for nearly a whole minute. The next thing they knew was that the Spaniel was gently waking them. The sun was already down, the fire dead, the room a little chilly. Pongo and Missis stretched sleepily.

"What you need is tea," said the Spaniel. "But first, a breath of air. Follow me."

There was still a faint glow from the sunset as they wandered round the wintry, tangled garden. As Pongo looked back towards the beautiful old red-brick house, the Spaniel told them it was four hundred years old and that nobody now lived there but himself, Sir Charles, and the valet, John. Most of the rooms were shut up.

"But we dust them sometimes," he said. "That's a very long walk for me."

The great window was lit by the flicker of firelight. "It's in there we sit, mostly," the Spaniel told them. "We should be warmer in one of the smaller rooms, but Sir Charles likes to be in the Great Hall." A silvery bell tinkled. "There! He's ringing for me. Tea's ready. Now, do just as I tell you."

He led them indoors and then into a large high room, at the far end of which was an enormous fire. In front of it sat an old gentleman, but they could not yet see him very well because there was a screen round the back of his chair.

"Please lie down at the back of the screen," whispered the Spaniel. "Later Sir Charles will fall asleep and you can come closer to the fire."

As Pongo and Missis tiptoed to the back of the screen, they noticed that there was a large table beside Sir Charles on which was his luncheon tray—finished with now, and neatly covered by a table-napkin—and everything necessary for tea. Water was already boiling in a silver kettle over a spirit lamp. Sir Charles filled the teapot and put the tea-cosy on. Then he lifted a silver cover from a plate on which there were a number of slices of bread. By now the Spaniel had joined him and was thumping his tail.

"Hungry, are you?" said Sir Charles. "Well, we've a good fire for our toast."

Then he put a slice of bread on a toasting fork. It was no ordinary toasting fork, for it was made of iron and nearly four feet long. It was really meant for pushing logs into position. But it was just what Sir Charles needed, and he handled it with great skill, avoiding the flaming logs and toasting the bread where the wood glowed red hot. A slice of toast was ready in no time. Sir Charles buttered it thickly and offered a piece to the Spaniel, who ate it while Sir Charles watched.

Missis was a little surprised that the courteous Spaniel had not offered her the first piece. She was even more surprised when he received a second piece and ate that too, while Sir Charles watched. She began to feel very hungry—and very anxious. Surely the kind Spaniel had not invited them to tea just to watch him eat? Then a third piece of toast was offered— and this time Sir Charles happened to turn away. Instantly the Spaniel dropped the toast behind the screen. Piece after piece travelled this way to Pongo and Missis, with the Spaniel only eating one now and then—when Sir Charles happened to be looking. Missis felt ashamed of her hungry suspicions.

"Never known you with such a good appetite, my boy," said the old gentleman delightedly. And he made slice after slice of toast until all the bread was gone. Then cakes were handed on in the same way. And then Sir Charles offered the Spaniel a silver bowl of tea. This was put down so close to the edge of the screen that Pongo and Missis were able to drink some while Sir Charles was looking the other way. When he saw

81

the bowl empty, he filled it again and again so everyone had enough. Pongo and Missis had always had splendid food, but they had never before had hot buttered toast and sweet milky tea. It was a meal they always remembered.

At last Sir Charles rose stiffly, put another log on the fire, and then settled back in his chair and closed his eyes. Soon he was asleep, and the Spaniel beckoned Pongo and Missis to the fire. They sat on the warm hearth and looked up at the old gentleman. His face was deeply lined and all the lines drooped, and somehow he had a look of the Spaniel—or the Spaniel had a look of Sir Charles. Both of them were lit by the firelight, and beyond them was the great window, now blue with evening.

We ought to be on our way," whispered Pongo to Missis. But it was so warm, so quiet, and they were both so full of buttered toast that they drifted into a light and delightful sleep.

Pongo awoke with a start. Surely someone had spoken his name?

The fire was no longer blazing brightly, but there was still enough light to see that the old gentleman was awake and leaning forward.

"Well, if that isn't Pongo and his missis," he murmured smilingly. "Well, Well! What a pleasure! What a pleasure!"

Missis had opened her eyes now.

The Spaniel whispered, "Don't move, either of you."

"Can *you* see them?" said the old gentleman, putting his hand on the Spaniel's head. "If you can, don't be frightened. They won't hurt you. You'd have liked them. Let's see, they must have died fifty years before you were born—more than that. They were the first dogs I ever knew. I used to ask my mother to stop the carriage and let them get inside—I couldn't bear to see them running behind. So in the end, they just became house dogs. How often they sat there in the firelight. Hey, you two! If dogs *can* come back, why haven't you come back before?"

Then Pongo knew that Sir Charles thought they were ghost dogs. And he remembered that Mr. Dearly had named him "Pongo" because it was a name given to many Dalmatians of those earlier days when they ran behind carriages. Sir Charles had taken him and Missis for Dalmatians he had known in his childhood.

"Probably my fault," the old gentleman went on. "I've never been what they call 'psychic' nowadays. This house is supposed to be full of ghosts, but *I've* never seen any. I dare say I'm only seeing you because I'm pretty close to the edge now— and quite time, too. I'm more than ready. Well, what a joy to know that dogs go on too—I've always hoped it. Good news for you too, my boy." He fondled the Spaniel's ears. "Well, Pongo and his pretty wife, after all these years! Can't see you so well now, but I shall remember!"

The fire was sinking lower and lower. They could no longer see the old gentleman's face, but soon his even breathing told them he was asleep again. The Spaniel rose quietly.

"Come with me now," he whispered, "for John will be back soon to get supper. You have given my dear old pet a great pleasure. I am deeply grateful."

They tiptoed out of the vast, dark hall and made their way to the kitchen, where the Spaniel pressed more food on them.

"Just a few substantial biscuits—my tin is always left open for me when John is away."

Then they had a last drink of water, and the Spaniel gave Pongo directions for reaching Suffolk. They were full of "rights" and "lefts," and Missis did not take in one word.

The Spaniel noticed her dazed look and said playfully, "Now which is your right paw?"

"One of the front ones," said Missis brightly. At which Pongo and the Spaniel laughed in a very masculine way.

Then they thanked the Spaniel and said good-bye. Missis said she would always remember that day.

"So shall I," said the Spaniel, smiling at her. "Ah, Pongo, what a lucky dog you are!"

"I know it," said Pongo, looking proudly at Missis.

Then they were off.

After they had been running across the fields for some minutes, Missis said anxiously, "How's your leg, Pongo?"

"Much, much better. Oh, Missis, I am ashamed of myself. I made such a fuss this morning. It was partly rage. Pain hurts more when one is angry. You were such a comfort to me— and so brave."

"And you were a comfort to me the night we left London," said Missis. "It will be all right as long as we never lose courage both together."

"I'm glad you did not let me bite that small human."

"*Nothing* should ever make a dog bite a human," said Missis in a virtuous voice.

Pongo remembered something. "You said only the night before last that you were going to tear Cruella de Vil to pieces."

"That is different," said Missis grimly. "I do not consider Cruella de Vil *is* human."

Thinking of Cruella made them anxious for the puppies,

84

and they ran on faster, without talking any more for a long time.

Then Missis said, "Pongo, how far away from the puppies are we now?"

"With good luck we should reach them tomorrow morning," said Pongo.

Just before midnight they came to the market town of Sudbury. Pongo paused as they crossed the bridge over the River Stour.

"Here we enter Suffolk," he said triumphantly.

They ran on through the quiet streets of old houses and into the market square. They had hoped they might meet some dog and hear if any news of the puppies had come at the Twilight Barking, but not so much as a cat was stirring. While they were drinking at the fountain, church clocks began to strike midnight.

Missis said gladly, "Oh, Pongo, it's tomorrow! Now we shall be with our puppies today!"

What They Saw
from the Folly

As the night wore on, they travelled through many pretty villages to a countryside wilder than any they had yet seen. There were more woods and heaths, fewer farms. So wild was it that Pongo would risk no short cuts and stuck cautiously to the roads, which were narrow and twisted. The moon was behind clouds, so he could not read what few signposts there were.

"I'm so afraid we may go through our village without knowing it," he said. "For as we have not been able to send any news by the Twilight Barking, nobody will be on the lookout for us."

But he was wrong. Suddenly, out of the darkness, came a loud "Miaow."

They stopped instantly. Just ahead of them, up a tree, was a tabby cat. She said, "Pongo and Missis? I suppose you *are* friendly?"

"Yes, indeed, madam," said Pongo. "Are you by any chance the cat who helped to find our puppies?"

"That's me," said the cat.

"Oh, thank you, thank you!" cried Missis.

The cat jumped down. "Sorry to seem suspicious of you, but some dogs just can't control themselves when they see a cat—not that *I've* ever had any trouble. Well, here you are."

"How very kind of you to keep watch for us, madam," said Pongo.

"No hardship, I'm usually out at night. You can call me Tib. My real name's Pussy Willow, but that's too long for most people—a pity, really, as it's a name I could fancy."

"It suits you so well," said Pongo in a courtly tone he had picked up from the Spaniel, "with your slender figure and soft grey paws." He was taking a chance in saying this, for it was too dark for him to see her figure, let alone her paws.

The cat was delighted. "Well, I have kept my figure—and it was my paws got me the name Pussy Willow. Now you'll be wanting a bite of food and a good long rest."

"Please tell us if all is still well with our puppies," said Missis.

"It was, yesterday afternoon—when I last saw them. Lively as crickets and fat as butter, they were."

87

"Could *we* see them—just a glimpse—before we eat or sleep?" asked Missis.

"We can't climb trees, as Mrs. Willow can," said Pongo.

"You won't need to," said the cat. "The Colonel's made other arrangements. But you can't see the puppies before they are let out for exercise, and that'll be hours yet. Those Badduns are late risers. Well, come along and meet the Colonel."

"A human Colonel?" asked Missis, puzzled.

"Bless me, no. The Colonel's our Sheepdog. A perfect master of strategy—you ask the sheep. He calls me his lieutenant."

The cat was now leading them along the road. Pongo asked how far it was to the farm.

"Oh, we're not going to the farm now. The Colonel's spending the night at the Folly. Crazy place, but it's coming in very useful."

The darkness was thinning. Soon the road ran across a stretch of heath on which, still some way ahead of them, a dark mass stood out against the gradually lightening sky. After a few moments Pongo saw that the dark mass was a great stone wall.

"There you are," said the cat. "Your puppies are behind that."

"It looks like the wall of a prison," said Pongo.

"*Nasty* place," said the cat. "The Colonel will tell you its history."

She led them from the road over the rough grass of the heath. As they drew nearer, Pongo saw that the wall curved— as the wall of a round tower curves. Above it rose the trunks of tall trees, their bare branches black against the sky.

"You'd think there would be a castle, at least, inside that huge wall," said the cat. "And they do say there was going to be, only something went wrong. All that's there now—Well, you can see for yourself."

She led the way to the rusty iron gates, and Pongo and Missis peered through the bars. There was now enough light for them to see some distance. Beyond a stretch of grass as wild as the surrounding heath, they saw the glint of water— but, strangely, it seemed to be *black* water. Then they saw the reason why. Reflected in it was a *black* house.

It was the most frightening house Pongo and Missis had ever seen. Many of the windows in its large, flat face had been bricked up and those that were left looked like eyes and a nose, with the front door for a mouth. Only there were too many eyes, and the nose and the mouth were not quite in the right places, so that the whole face looked distorted.

"It's seen us!" gasped Missis—and it really did seem as if the eyes of the house were staring at them from its cracked and peeling black face.

"Well, that's Hell Hall for you," said the cat.

She moved on and they followed her, round the curving wall. After a few minutes they saw a tower rising high above the tree-tops. It was built of rough grey stone, like the wall, and was rather like a church tower. But there was no church. The tower simply jutted out of the wall. Some of the narrow windows were broken, and their stonework was crumbling. The place was not yet a ruin but looked as if it quite soon might be one.

"Well may they call it a Folly!" said the cat.

Missis did not know what the word meant, but Pongo had

seen a Folly before and was able to explain. The name is often given to expensive, odd buildings built for no sensible reason, buildings that it was a foolishness to build.

The cat miaowed three times, and there were three answering barks from inside the tower. A moment later came the sound of a bolt being drawn back.

"The Colonel's the only dog I ever knew who could manage bolts with his teeth," said the cat proudly.

Pongo instantly decided *he* would learn to manage bolts.

"Come in, come in," said a rumbling voice, "but let me have a look at you first. There's not much light inside yet."

An enormous Sheepdog came out. Pongo saw at once that this was none of your dapper military men but a lumbering old soldier man, possibly a slow thinker but widely experienced. His eyes glittered shrewdly and kindly through his masses of grey-and-white woolly hair.

"Glad to see you're *large* Dalmatians," he said approvingly. "I've nothing against small dogs, but the size of all breeds should be kept up. Well, now, what's been happening to you? There was a rare to-do on the Twilight Barking last night, when no one had any news of you."

He led the way into the Folly, while Pongo told of their day with the Spaniel.

"Sounds a splendid fellow," said the Colonel. "Sorry he's not on the Barking. Now, tuck in, you two. I provided breakfast just in case you turned up."

There was plenty of good farmhouse food and a deep round tin full of water.

"How did you get it all here?" asked Pongo astonished.

"I rolled the round tin from the farm—with the food inside

it," said the Colonel. "I stuffed the tin with straw so that the food wouldn't fall out. And then I borrowed a small seaside bucket from my young pet, Tommy—the dear little chap would lend me anything. I can carry that bucket by its handle. Six trips to the pond on the heath got the water here—lucky it thawed yesterday. Drink up! Plenty more where that came from."

The cat acted as hostess during the meal. Pongo was careful always to address her as "Mrs. Willow."

"What's this Mrs. Willow business?" said the Colonel suddenly.

"Pussy Willow happens to be my given name," said the cat. "And I'm certainly a Mrs."

"You've got too many names," said the Colonel. "You're 'Puss' because all cats are 'Puss.' You're 'Pussy Willow' because it's your given name. You're 'Tib' because most people call you that. *I* call you 'Lieutenant' or 'Lieutenant Tib.' I thought you liked it."

"I like 'Lieutenant' but not 'Lieutenant Tib.' "

"Well, you can't be '*Mrs.* Willow' on top of everything else. You can't have six names."

"I'm entitled to *nine* names as I've nine lives," said the cat. "But I'll settle for 'Lieutenant Willow'—with 'Puss' for playful moments."

"Right," said the Colonel. "And now we'll show our guests their sleeping quarters."

"Oh, please," begged Missis. "Couldn't we get just a glimpse of the puppies before we sleep?"

The cat shot a quick look at the Colonel and said, "I've told them the pups won't be out for hours yet."

"Besides, you'd get too excited to sleep," said the Colonel. "You must both have a good rest before you start worrying."

"Worrying?" said Pongo sharply. "Is something wrong?"

"I give you my word there is nothing wrong with your puppies," said the Colonel.

Pongo and Missis believed him—and yet they both thought there was something odd about his voice, and about the look the cat had given him.

"Now up we go," the Colonel went on briskly. "You're sleeping on the top floor because that's the only floor where the windows aren't broken. Want a ride Lieutenant Wib—I mean Lieutenant Tillow—oh, good heavens, cat!"

"If there's one thing I object to being called, it's plain 'cat,' " said the cat.

"Quite right. I don't like being called plain 'dog,' " said the Colonel. "I apologize, Lieutenant Willow. Now jump on my back unless you want to walk."

The cat jumped on the Colonel's back and held on by his long hair. Pongo had never before seen a cat jump on a dog's back with friendly intentions. He was deeply impressed—both by the Colonel's trustfulness and the cat's trustworthiness.

The narrow, twisting stairs went up through five floors of the Folly, most of them full of broken furniture, old trunks, and all manner of rubbish. On the top floor was a deep bed of straw, brought up by the Colonel in a sack. But what interested Missis far more was the narrow window—surely it must look towards Hell Hall?

She ran to see. Yes, beyond the tree-tops and a neglected orchard was the back of the black house—which was as ugly as the front, though it did not have such a frightening

93

expression. At one side was a large stableyard.

"Is that where the puppies will come out?" she asked.

"Yes, yes," said the Colonel, "but it won't be for—well, for some time yet."

"I shall never sleep until I've seen them," said Missis.

"Yes, you will, because I shall *talk* you to sleep," said the Colonel. "Your husband has asked me to tell him the history of Hell Hall. Now come and lie down."

Pongo was as anxious to see the puppies as Missis was, but he knew they should sleep first, so he coaxed her to lie down. The Colonel pulled the straw round both of them.

"It's chilly in here—not that *I* feel it," he said. Then he sent the cat to start collecting food for the next meal, and began to talk in his rumbling voice. This was the story he told.

Hell Hall had once been an ordinary farmhouse named Hill Hall—it had been built by a farmer named Hill. It was about two hundred years old, the same age as the farm where the Sheepdog and the cat lived.

"The two houses are quite a bit alike," said the Colonel, "only our place is painted white and well cared for. I remember Hell Hall before it was painted black and it really wasn't bad at all."

The farmer named Hill had got into debt and sold Hill Hall to an ancestor of Cruella de Vil's, who liked its lonely position on the wild heath. He intended to pull the farmhouse down and build himself a fantastic house which was to be a mixture of a castle and a cathedral, and had begun by building the surrounding wall and the Folly. (The Colonel had heard all this while visiting the Vicarage.)

Once the wall, with its heavy iron gates, was finished,

94

strange rumours began to spread. Villagers crossing the heath at night heard screams and wild laughter. Were there prisoners behind the prison-like wall? People began to count their children carefully.

"Some of the stories—Well, I shan't tell you just as you're falling asleep," said the Colonel. "I didn't hear *them* at the Vicarage. But I will tell you something—because it won't upset you as it naturally upset the villagers. It was said that this de Vil fellow had a long tail. I didn't hear that at the Vicarage, either."

Missis had taken in very little of this and was now fast asleep, but Pongo was keenly interested.

"By this time," the Colonel went on, "people were calling the place *Hell* Hall, and the de Vil chap plain devil. The end came when the men from several villages arrived one night with lighted torches, prepared to break open the gates and burn the farmhouse down. But as they approached the gates a terriffic thunderstorm began and put the torches out. Then the gates burst open—seemingly of their own accord—and out came de Vil, driving a coach and four. And the story is that lightning was coming not from the skies but from de Vil—blue forked lightning. All the men ran away screaming and never came back. And neither did de Vil. The house stood empty for thirty years. Then someone rented it. It's been rented again and again, but no one ever stays."

"And it still belongs to the de Vil family?" asked Pongo.

"There's only Cruella de Vil left of the family now. Yes, she owns it. She came down here some years ago and had the house painted black. It's red inside, I'm told. But she never lived here. She lets the Baddun brothers have it rent free, as caretakers. I wouldn't let them take care of any kennel of mine."

Those were the last words Pongo heard, for, as the story ended, sleep wrapped him round. The Sheepdog stood looking down at the peaceful couple.

"Well, *they're* in for a shock," he thought, and then lumbered his way downstairs.

It was less than an hour later when Missis opened her eyes. She had been dreaming of the puppies, she had heard them barking—and they *were* barking! She sprang out of the straw and dashed to the window. No pup was to be seen, but she could hear the barking clearly—it was coming from inside the black house. Then the barking grew louder, the door to the stableyard opened, and out came a stream of puppies.

Missis blinked. Surely her puppies could not have grown so much in less than a week? And surely she had not had so *many* puppies? More and more were hurrying out; the whole yard was filling up with fine, large, healthy Dalmatian puppies, but—

Missis raised her head in a wail of despair. These puppies were not hers at all! The whole thing was a mistake! *Her* puppies were still lost, perhaps starving, perhaps even dead. Again and again she howled in anguish.

Her first howl had wakened Pongo. He was beside her in a couple of seconds and staring at the yard full of milling, tumbling puppies. And they were *still* coming out of the house, rather smaller puppies now—

And then they saw him—smaller, even, than they had remembered. Lucky! There was no mistaking that horseshoe of spots on his back. And after him came Roly Poly, falling over his feet as usual. Then Patch and the tiny Cadpig and all the others—all well, all lashing their tails, all eager to drink at the low troughs of water that stood about in the yard.

"Look, Patch is helping the Cadpig to find a place," said Missis delightedly. "But what does it mean? Where have all those other puppies come from?"

Dazed as he was with sleep, Pongo's keen brain had gone into instant action. He saw it all. Cruella must have begun stealing puppies months before—soon after that evening when she had said she would like a Dalmatian fur coat. The largest pups in the yard looked at least five months old. Then they went down and down in size. Smallest and youngest of all were his own puppies, which must obviously have been the last to be stolen.

He had barely finished explaining this to Missis when the Sheepdog reached the top of the stairs—he had been downstairs getting in fresh water and had heard Missis howl.

"Well, now you know," he said. "I was hoping you could have had your sleep out first."

"But why are you both looking so worried?" asked Missis. "Our puppies are safe and well."

"Yes, my dear. You go on watching them," said Pongo gently. Then he turned to the Colonel.

You come downstairs and have a drink, my boy," said the Colonel.

In the Enemy's Camp

Oh, how Pongo needed that drink!

"And now stroll down to the pond with me," said the Colonel, gripping the handle of a little tin bucket in his teeth. "You won't feel like trying to sleep any more just at present."

Pongo felt he would never be able to sleep again.

"I blame myself for letting you in for this shock," said the Colonel as they went out into the early morning sunlight. "Because you can't blame the Lieutenant. She's not a trained observer. When she told me the place was 'seething with Dalmatian puppies' I naturally thought she meant *your* puppies only. After all, fifteen puppies can do quite a bit of seething. It was only yesterday, after I'd made the Folly my headquarters and could see over the wall, that I found out the true facts. Of course I sent the news over yesterday's Twilight Barking but couldn't reach you."

"How many puppies are there?" asked Pongo.

"Can't tell, exactly, because they never keep still. But I'd say—counting yours—getting on for a hundred."

"A *hundred?*"

They had reached the pond. "Have another drink," suggested the Colonel.

Pongo gulped down some more water, then stared hopelessly at the Sheepdog.

"Colonel, what am I going to do?"

"Will your lady wife want just to rescue her own puppies?"

"She may at first," said Pongo. "But not when she realizes it would mean leaving all the others to certain death."

"Anyway, your pups aren't old enough for the journey," said the Colonel. "I suppose you know that?"

Pongo did know it. His plan had been to let his puppies stay at Hell Hall until they were a little bigger, while he and Missis kept watch over them, ready to rescue them if danger threatened. He told the Colonel this.

"And that's exactly what you must do," said the Colonel.

"But what about the other puppies?"

"I shall spread the news of them throughout England. Other parents may come to the rescue."

"I doubt it, after all this time," said Pongo.

"If the worst comes to the worst, would your pets give them a home?"

99

Pongo couldn't imagine the Dearlys refusing to help any dog. But getting on for a hundred! Still, the drawing room was very large.

"I don't believe they'd turn them away," he said. "But, Colonel, I could never get the whole lot of them to London."

"Not as they are, of course. Every dog jack of them has to be trained. They must learn to march, to obey orders—I may teach the bigger ones how to forage."

"I wouldn't mind learning that myself," said Pongo.

"Splendid! Now how about trying your mouth at carrying this pail? That's a trick you ought to learn. No, no—hold your head farther out. Then the pail won't bang into your chest. Excellent!"

Pongo found that he could carry the bucket of water quite easily. His spirits were rising now. With this wonderful old Colonel to help him, he would rescue *every* puppy. He set the bucket down in the Folly.

"You're looking better," said the Colonel. "You may be able to sleep now. There's nothing more you and your lady can do until it's dark. Then you shall meet your family. Meanwhile, I'll send in word that you've arrived."

Something was puzzling Pongo. "Colonel, why did Cruella steal so *many* Dalmatians? She can't want more than *one* Dalmatian fur coat?"

The Sheepdog looked astonished. "Surely you know her husband's a furrier? I understand she only married him for his furs."

So that was it! Pongo had forgotten. But if the de Vils planned to sell Dalmatian coats to the public, then Hell Hall was nothing less than a Dalmatian fur farm and no Dalmatian would ever be safe again unless Cruella's career came to an end. "I must cope with that when I get back to London," thought Pongo grimly as he mounted the stairs.

He found Missis stretched out on the bare boards by the window. She had watched until the puppies had all gone in, then toppled into sleep. He pulled straw around her and lay down very close, to keep her warm. She did not stir. His last waking thoughts were humble ones. He had expected the Sheepdog to be some doddering old country gaffer. How much now depended on this shrewd, kind old soldier!

It was dark when the Colonel woke them.

"All still well with the pups, but no news of any other parents over the Twilight Barking. I sent word of your safe arrival, and good wishes to you came pouring in. All Dogdom awaits news from this quiet village. I've said you'll bark a few words yourself when you're fully rested."

"Willingly," said Pongo.

"Now down we go to dinner," said the Colonel.

They went down and had an excellent meal of sausages which the cat had collected during the day. She was away at the farm—the Colonel said there would be hurt feelings if she did not join her pets at tea, to drink a saucer of milk. "And I must go back later, because my young pet, Tommy, likes me there while he has his bath. So let's be moving."

He rose and pushed open a window. "The defences of Hell Hall are childish," he said. "What's the use of padlocked gates at the front when one can get in at the back, through this Folly?"

Pongo then saw that the Folly had a door and a window opening onto the grounds of Hell Hall as well as the door and window opening onto the heath, and was, indeed a sort of gatehouse. The Colonel had originally entered through the window on the heath side. The door into the grounds was bolted on the Hell Hall side, so the Colonel led Pongo and Missis through the window.

"Now we'll be cautious," he said. "That window might blow shut, and there's no handle on the outside. And it might take some time to unbolt this door." He drew back the bolt on the door into the Folly, pushed the door open, and rolled a heavy stone against it. "Now, if you *should* want to get out in a hurry—But I don't think you will. Shouldn't wonder if you couldn't spend the night with your pups."

Missis gasped with delight and began to ask questions.

"I'll explain as we go," said the Colonel, starting towards Hell Hall.

A full moon was rising above the black house.

"Colonel, what's that on the roof?" said Pongo. "Surely it isn't *television*—here?"

"Oh, yes, it is," said the Colonel. "And there's scarcely a cottage in the village hasn't got it since the electricity came. Mostly on the Hire Purchase—though there won't be much Purchase here. I'm told the Badduns haven't paid anything for months."

He then outlined his plans, and it soon appeared that television played an important part in them. The Baddun brothers were so fond of it that they could not bear any puppy to bark while it was on. And unless the puppies were warm, they barked like mad. The warmest room in the house was the kitchen—which was where the television set was—so that was where the pups now lived (unless they were taking exercise in

102

the stableyard). Some pups liked watching the television, some just slept; anyway, none of them barked, so the Badduns could enjoy themselves in peace. All this the Colonel had heard from Lucky during long, barked conversations.

"That lad of yours is as bright as a button," said the Colonel. "He's months ahead of his age."

Pongo and Missis swelled with pride.

The plan was that Lucky should bring his brothers and sisters out to the stableyard while the Badduns were watching television.

"But it will be too cold for them to stay out long," said the Colonel, "and I don't see why you shouldn't go back into the kitchen with them. Lucky tells me there's no light except from the T.V. screen, so if you crunch down you should be quite safe. Even if the Badduns do see you, they'll just think you're two of the larger pups. But there's hardly any chance you will be seen because Lucky tells me the Badduns stay glued to the T.V. until it ends and then roll over and go to sleep—they've got mattresses on the kitchen floor. I see no reason why you shouldn't spend the night there. I'll call you at dawn and you can get out before the Badduns wake."

Pongo and Missis thought this was a wonderful idea.

"Can we sleep there every night?" asked Missis.

The Colonel said he hoped so and that it was at night that the pups would have to be drilled and trained for their march to London.

"Lucky says nothing wakes the Badduns, so *I* plan to come into the kitchen. I shall hold classes there and drill ten pups at a time in the stableyard. But you two must spend a quiet night there first and report conditions to me."

By now they were almost at the stableyard.

"Don't tell me any more now, Colonel," said Pongo. "I'm too excited to take it in. Are you all right, Missis?"

For Missis was trembling. "I can't believe I'm really going to see them," she said.

The Colonel opened the gate to the stableyard. Missis gave a soft moan and hurled herself across the yard. She had seen Lucky. There he stood, at the back door, waiting for them.

And behind him, in the long, dark passage leading to the kitchen, were all his brothers and sisters. Who could describe what the mother and father felt during the next few minutes, as they tried to cuddle fifteen wagging, wriggling, licking puppies all at once? Everyone tried to be quiet, but there were so many whimpers of bliss, so much happy snuffling, that the Sheepdog got nervous.

"Will they hear in there?" he asked Lucky.

"What, the Badduns?" said Lucky—rather indistinctly, because he had his mother's ear in his mouth. "No, they've got their precious television on extra loud."

Still, the Colonel was relieved when the first joy of the meeting was over.

"Quiet, now!" said Pongo.

"Quiet as mice!" said Missis.

But they were pleasantly surprised at how quiet the pups instantly were. The only sound came from some dead leaves stirred by fifteen lashing little tails.

"Now, still!" said Lucky.

All the tails stopped wagging.

"I'm teaching them to obey orders," said Lucky to the Colonel.

104

"Good boy, good boy. Let's see, I made you a Corporal this afternoon, didn't I? I now make you a Sergeant. If all goes well, you shall have your commission next week. Now I'm off to see my little pet, Tommy, have his bath."

He told Pongo he would be back in a couple of hours. "Slip out and tell me what you think of things—or send the Sergeant with a message."

"Won't you come in and see the T.V., sir?" said Lucky.

"Not while the Badduns are awake," said the Colonel. "Even *they* couldn't mistake me for a Dalmatian."

As soon as he had gone, Lucky sent the other puppies to the kitchen, then took his father and mother in.

"You must stay at the back until your eyes get used to the dark," he said.

And indeed it was dark! The only light came from the television screen and the kitchen fire, which were at opposite ends of the very large kitchen. And as the walls and ceiling were painted dark red, they reflected no light. It was extremely warm—much warmer than one fire could have made it. This was because there was central heating. Cruella de Vil had put it in when she planned to live in the house.

At last Pongo and Missis found they could see fairly well, and it was a strange sight they saw. Only a few feet away from the television, two men lay sprawled on old mattresses, their eyes fixed on the screen. Behind them were ranged row after row of puppies, small pups at the front, large pups at the back. Those who did not care for television were asleep round the kitchen fire. The hot, red room was curiously cosy, though Pongo felt it was a bit like being inside a giant's mouth.

Lucky whispered, "I thought we could settle Mother with

106

the family and then I could show you round a bit. All the pups want to get a glimpse of you. Father, you are going to rescue them *all*?"

"I hope so," said Pongo earnestly—wondering more and more how he was going to manage it.

"I told them you would, but they've been pretty nervous. I'll just send the word round that they can count on you." He whispered to a pup at the end of a row, and the word travelled like wind over a cornfield. There was barely a sound that a human ear could have heard, except a couple of tail thumps, instantly repressed. All knew they must not give away the fact that Pongo was in their midst, and when he went silently along the rows there was scarcely a movement. But he could feel great waves of love and trust rolling towards him. And suddenly all the pups were real and living for him, not just a problem he had to face. He felt as if he were the father of them all. And he knew that he could never desert them.

He felt a special sympathy for the big pups in the two back rows. Some of them were fully half-grown—young dogs rather than puppies, lollopy creatures with clumsy feet. They made him remember his own not very far-away youth. He wondered how long their skins would be safe from Cruella—would she have the patience to wait much longer? Did the big pups know that danger drew close every day? Something in their eyes told him they did. And many of them had been in this horrible place for months, without hope until Lucky had spread the news that his father and mother were coming. Proud Lucky now, taking his father along the rows of hero-worshipping pups!

Blissfully happy, Missis sat with her children clustered about

107

her. She had eyes only for them, but they were determined she should not miss the television. She had never seen it before (Mr. and Mrs. Dearly did not care for it) and found it difficult to follow. The pups did not follow it completely, as they had not yet learned enough human words; but they liked the little moving figures, and watched in the perpetual hope of seeing dogs on the screen.

"Can we have it when we get back home?" said the Cadpig.

"Indeed you shall, my darling," said Missis. Somehow, somehow, the Dearlys must be made to buy a set.

Pongo had now silently "met" all the pups. He told Lucky he would like to have a good look at the Badduns. So Lucky took him a little way up the back staircase, where they could see without being noticed.

No one would have guessed that Saul and Jasper Baddun were brothers. Saul was heavy and dark, with a forehead so low that his bushy eyebrows often got tangled with his matted hair. Jasper was thin and fair, with a chin so sharp and pointed that it had worn holes in all his shirts—not that he had many. Both brothers looked very dirty.

"They never change their awful old clothes," whispered Lucky, "and they never wash. I don't think they are real humans, Father. Is there such a thing as a half-human?"

Pongo could well believe it after seeing the Badduns, but he couldn't imagine what their non-humans half was. It was no animal he had ever seen.

"Have they ill-treated any of you?" he asked anxiously.

"No, they're too frightened of being bitten," said Lucky. "They're terrible cowards. Some of the big pups did think of attacking them—but there seemed no way of getting out. And if they'd killed the Badduns, there would have been no one to feed us. Oh, Father, how glad I am you've come!"

Pongo licked his son's ear. Pups, like boys, do not like fathers to be too sentimental (mothers are different), but this was a very private moment.

Then they went and sat with Missis and the family. It seemed strange that they could all be so peaceful right in the enemy's camp. Gradually the Pongos' puppies fell asleep— all except Lucky, Patch, and the Cadpig. Lucky was not sleepy. Patch was—but stayed awake because the Cadpig was awake. And the Cadpig stayed awake because she was crazy about television.

Many of the big pups, too, were lying down to sleep, stretching luxuriously, feeling—for the first time since they had been imprisoned in Hell Hall—that there was someone they could rely on. Pongo had come! And Missis too. They had looked at her shyly, quite understanding that she must care for her own children first, but hoping she would have a little time for them later. Some of them could hardly remember their mothers. But the younger pups could remember theirs and they were not sleeping. Slowly, silently, they were inching their way towards Missis.

She had been watching the television, beginning to get the hang of it, with the Cadpig's help. Then some tiny sound, close at hand, brought her attention back to her family. But the sound had not come from her family. There were now nearly thirty puppies, not so very much bigger than her own, just a few feet away, all staring at her hopefully.

"Goodness, they're grubby," was her first thought. "Didn't their mothers teach them to wash themselves?"

109

Then she felt a pang of pity. What mother had any of them now? She smiled at them all—and they wrinkled their little noses in a return smile. Then she looked beyond then, to the larger pups. Some of the half-grown girls reminded her of herself at their age—so slim, so silly. They knew how to wash themselves but there were many things they didn't know, many ways in which they needed a mother's advice. And suddenly all the puppies were her puppies; she was their mother—just as Pongo had felt he was their father. And indeed the younger ones creeping closer and closer to her were now so mingled with her own that she could scarcely tell where her little family ended and her larger family began.

Drowsiness spread throughout the warm red room. Even the Baddun brothers dozed. They did not much like the programme that was on the television and wanted to be fresh for their very favourite programme, which was due later. Even Missis slept a little, knowing that Pongo would keep watch. At last only three pairs of eyes were open. Pongo was wide awake, thinking, thinking. Lucky was wide awake, for he thought of himself as a sentry, who must not sleep on duty. And the Cadpig was wide awake, watching her lovely, lovely television.

Suddenly there was a thunder of thumps on the front door. The sleeping pups awoke in alarm. The Baddun brothers lumbered to their feet and stumbled towards the door. But before they got there it had been flung open.

Outside, against the moonlit sky stood a figure in a long white cloak.

It was Cruella de Vil.

Sudden Danger

For a few seconds she stared into the dimly lit room. Then she shouted, "Saul! Jasper! Turn off that television! And turn on the light!"

"We can't turn on the light because we've no electric bulbs left," said Saul Baddun. "When the telly finishes, we go to bed."

"And if we turn the telly off, there'll be no light at all," said Jasper Baddun.

"Well, turn the sound off, anyway," said Cruella, angrily.

Jasper did as he was told, and the little figures moving on the screen were suddenly voiceless. The Cadpig yapped indignantly. Missis, who was crouching low in the midst of her family, instantly hushed her. Pongo, also crouched low, got ready to spring at Cruella if she attacked any pup. But she seemed scarcely to notice any of them. Those near her shrank back as she strode into the room.

"I've got a job for you, my lads," she said to the Badduns. "The pups must be killed tonight—every single one of them."

The Badduns gaped at her. "But they're not big enough to be made into fur coats yet," said Saul.

"The largest ones are, and the little ones can be made into gloves. Anyway, they've got to die—before someone finds them. There's been so much in the papers about the Dearlys' dogs. All England's on the hunt for Dalmatians."

"But how could anyone find them here?" said Jasper Baddun. "Why can't they just stay on, growing bigger and bigger?"

"It's too risky," said Cruella. "Someone might hear them yapping and tell the police. My husband's going to ship the skins abroad—except the ones I keep for my own coat. I shall have it reversible—Persian lamb one side and Dalmatian dog the other—and wear the dog inside until people forget about the Dearlys' pups. When that happens, I'll collect another lot and we'll start our Dalmatian fur farm again. But this lot must be got rid of—quickly."

"How?" said the Badduns, both together.

"Any way you like. Poison them, drown them, hit them on the head. Have you any chloroform in the larder?"

"Not a drop," said Saul Baddun. "And no ether, either."

"We can't afford luxuries, growled Jasper Baddun.

"Drown them, then."

"Dogs can swim," said Saul Baddun. "Anyway, the pond's less than a foot deep."

"Then you must hit them on the head," said Cruella.

Saul Baddun had gone pale. "What, hit ninety-seven pups on the head?" he said shakily. "We couldn't do it. Have pity, Mrs. de Vil. We'd be wore out."

"Listen," said Cruella de Vil. "*I* don't care *how* you kill the little beasts. Hang them, suffocate them, drop them off the roof—good gracious, there are dozens of lovely ways. I only wish I'd time to do the job myself."

"Couldn't you make time, Mrs. de Vil?" said Jasper. "You'd do it so beautifully—it'd be a pleasure to watch you."

Cruella shook her head. "I've got to get back to London." Then a fiendish look came into her eyes. "Here's an idea for you. Shut them up without food, and then they'll kill each other."

"But they'd make such a horrible noise about it," said Saul Baddun. "We'd never be able to hear the telly."

"Besides, they'd damage each other's skins," said Cruella. "That would ruin their value. You must kill them *carefully*. Then you can start the skinning."

"But *we* can't skin them!" wailed Jasper. "We don't know how."

"My husband will show you," said Cruella. "We'll both drive down tomorrow night. And we shall count the bodies—just remember that, will you? If you've let even one pup escape, I'll turn you out of Hell Hall. Now you'd better get busy. Good night."

Fortunately, few of the pups knew enough Human to understand Cruella's words fully, but they all felt she was evil. And as she made her way to the door she aimed a kick at a small pup who was dangerously close to her. It was more frightened than hurt, but it gave a loud wail of anguish. Several of the bigger pups snarled indignantly at Cruella. Lucky, remembering the time he had nibbled her ear, barked out hastily, "Don't bite her, chaps She tastes hot!"

So Cruella got to the door unhurt. She flung it open, and the moonlight shone on her black-and-white hair and her absolutely simple white mink cloak. Then she looked back at the roomful of puppies.

"Good-bye, you horrid little beasts," she said. "I shall like you so much better when you're skins instead of pups. And I shall simply love the ones who are made into my own coat. *How* I'm looking forward to it!"

They saw her walk out past the pond which reflected the black house, and on to the great iron gates, which she unlocked and locked again behind her. Then, through the silent winter night, came the sound of a powerful car driving away, followed by one strident blast from the loudest motor-horn in England.

How well Pongo and Missis remembered that terrifying sound! It took them back to the happy evening when they had stood beside the striped black-and-white car on the Outer Circle. How safe and contented they had been then, little guessing what dangers lay ahead!

Jasper Baddun hurriedly shut the front door, saying, "If we've got to do the pups in, we'd better keep them all in one place."

Pongo felt stunned. If only he could think! If only the Sheepdog were there to advise him!

Missis whispered, "If you wish to attack those villains, I will help you, Pongo."

Lucky said quickly, "They always carry knives."

Pongo's brain was beginning to work. "If we attack them, they may kill us," he whispered to Missis. "And then there will be no one to help the pups. Quiet! Let me think."

The Badduns were talking together in low grunts.

"One thing's certain," said Jasper. "We can't do it tonight or we shall miss 'What's My Crime?' "

It was their very favourite television programme. Two ladies and two gentlemen, in faultless evening dress, had to guess the crime committed by a lady or gentleman in equally fault-less evening dress. Stern moralists said this programme was causing a crime wave and filling the prisons, because people committed crimes in the hope of being chosen as contestants. But crime is usually waving and the prisons are usually full, so probably "What's My Crime?" had not made much dif-ference. Both the Badduns longed to appear as contestants, but they knew they would never be chosen unless they com-mitted a really *original* crime, and they had never been able to think of one.

"We could kill the pups *after* 'What's My Crime?' Jasper," said Saul. "We ought to do it tonight, while they're sleepy. They'll be more dangerous when they're wide awake."

"It's a nuisance, that's what it is," said Jasper. "And whatever way we do it, we shall be *exhausted*. First the killing and then the skinning!"

"Maybe we'll get the knack of the skinning," said Saul. "Then we can skin while we watch the telly."

"Still, ninety-seven pups!" said Jasper. Then a wild gleam came into his eyes. "Saul, I bet no one else has ever murdered ninety-seven Dalmatians. It might do the trick for us! It might get us onto 'What's My Crime?' "

116

"*Now* you're talking!" said Saul Baddun. "You and me, in evening dress with carnations in our buttonholes—and all England watching us. But we must think out some really striking way of doing our crime. Could we skin them *alive?*"

"They'd never keep still," said Jasper. "What about *boiling* them?"

Pongo whispered to Missis, "We shall have to attack. It's our only hope."

"I'll get the biggest pups to help you," said Lucky quietly. "We'll all help. I can bite quite well."

And then—something happened! The Cadpig, whose eyes were fixed on the silent television screen, gave three short, sharp barks. No human ear would have known that those barks meant "What's My Crime?" but the Baddun brothers, startled by the noise, looked towards the Cadpig and, in doing so, noticed the television screen. Saul Baddun let out a roar of rage; Jasper Baddun gave a howl of misery. It was on! "What's My Crime?"—but without any sound, of course. They were missing it, their favourite of all programmes, and just when for the first time they had hopes of appearing on it! They hurled themselves at the television set. Saul turned the sound on full blast. Jasper adjusted the picture. Then they flung themselves down on their mattresses, grunting with delight.

"They won't stir for the next half-hour," whispered Lucky.

At last Pongo's brain sprang into full action! Instantly he whispered to Lucky, "March the pups out to the stableyard! Your mother and I will mount guard over the Badduns."

Lucky whispered, "If we could go out through the larder,

117

we could eat tomorrow's breakfast on our way. That's the door—by the fireplace. It's bolted, but I expect you can unbolt it, can't you, Father?"

Pongo had never even tried to unbolt a door, but he had seen the Sheepdog do it. "Yes, Lucky," he said firmly. "I can unbolt it."

They tiptoed across the kitchen. Then Pongo stood on his hind legs and took the bolt in his teeth. It would not budge. He rested his teeth and took a good look at the bolt in the light from the fire. He saw the knob was turned down and would have to be raised before the bolt would slide.

"*Now* we shan't be long," he said to Lucky, and again took the knob in his teeth. He raised it, tried to slide it. Still it would not slide. He thought, "Lucky will lose confidence in me," and he dragged and dragged until he thought his teeth would break. Then he began to fear that if the bolt did shoot back it would make a loud noise. Just then there was a burst of applause from the television—someone had guessed a contestant. (He had stolen two hundred bath plugs from hotels.) Pongo made a desperate effort. The bolt shot back. The larder door swung open.

"I knew you'd do it, Father," said Lucky proudly.

"Just a matter of knowing how," said Pongo, running his tongue round his teeth to make sure they were all still there.

A cold draught came from the larder. It had been the dairy when Hell Hall was a farm, and there were wooden slats instead of windows. The moonlight, shining in through the slats, made bright stripes on the stone floor. Meat for the puppies' breakfast was already set out in long troughs—because the Badduns hated working in the early morning. There were

118

small troughs for the little pups and big ones for the larger pups.

Pongo said to Lucky, "Wait until I get back to your mother. Then, while she and I stand ready to attack the Badduns, march all the pups in here. Tell them no pup is to eat until the last pup has a place at a trough. I will join you then and give the word to start eating."

It was remarkable how quickly the pups left the kitchen, under Seageant Lucky's whispered directions. Row after row marched out, like children leaving a school hall after prayers, except that the big pups left first, as they were nearest the door. Pongo and Missis watched the Badduns anxiously, for the hundreds of little toenails made a clitter-clatter on the kitchen floor, and there were a few scuffles, snuffles, and snorts—though never even the smallest bark, for the pups guessed that their lives depended on their silence. But the Badduns had eyes and ears for nothing but television.

Lucky left his own brothers and sisters to the last—and last of all to leave was the Cadpig. She was an intelligent little puppy and quite understood that she had to escape, but oh, how she hated leaving the television! She went out backwards, still staring at the screen.

Then Pongo and Missis sped swiftly and silently across the big red kitchen. They looked back from the larder door and saw that the Badduns had not stirred.

"How much longer will 'What's My Crime?' last?" whispered Pongo.

"Twenty minutes," said the Cadpig promptly and wistfully.

Pongo and Missis closed the larder door. The bolt on the inside was low down and easy to manage. Pongo shot it home at once, while the pups looked on admiringly. Every pup had its place at a trough, but not one lick of food had been eaten.

"One, two, three—feed!" commanded Pongo.

In fifty-nine seconds flat every scrap of food had been eaten.

"But what about you and Mother?" said Lucky. "I think I can find the Badduns' Sunday dinner."

He found it on a shelf—two steaks, rather poor grade, but Pongo and Missis swiftly ate them. The Pongo gave troops the right to forage and led a search through the larder. Everything eatable was eaten, the big pups sharing with the little pups most fairly.

"Anything in tht cupboard?" said Pongo at last.

"Only coke for the central-heating furnace," said Lucky. "Well, the Badduns won't find anything to eat tomorrow, will they?"

"Let them eat coke," said Pongo.

The entire meal had taken nearly five minutes. Pongo now felt he must get his troops out of Hell Hall as fast as possible. There had been no time to think out plans for the future— he was counting on the Colonel's advice. All that could be done now was to lead the pups to the Folly. The outer door of the larder was easily opened; then across the old orchard they went and in at the door which the Colonel had so thought-fully propped open. Missis gave one backward glance at black Hell Hall under the full moon. What would the Badduns do when they found not one pup in the kitchen?

There was not room for ninety-seven pups on the ground floor of the Folly, nor would there have been in the crowded upstairs rooms, so Pongo marched everyone out onto the heath. As the last pup marched out, the Sheepdog arrived.

At first he thought Pongo had recklessly begun the escape too soon, but when he heard the true facts he praised Pongo highly and was particularly pleased that all pups had been fed before escaping.

"That was Sergeant Lucky's idea," said Pongo proudly.

"Good work, Sergeant-*Major*," said the Colonel.

"But where are we to go?" asked Missis anxiously. "Look, the puppies are shivering."

They were indeed, for though it was not freezing it seemed terribly cold to them all after the warm kitchen.

The Sheepdog looked worried—not that anyone could see this, as his expressions were always hidden by hair. What was he to do, at a moment's notice, with ninety-seven Dalmatian puppies and two full-grown Dalmatians? At last he said, "Our big barn for the night, anyway. Pups can keep warm in the straw. It's only half a mile across the heath."

Half a mile! How little to Pongo and Missis! How much, how terribly much to the tiny Cadpig! After even a few hundred yards, Pongo was in despair about the long journey to London which lay ahead.

The big pups ran along happily. The medium-sized pups did quite well. Even most of the smaller pups looked as if they were capable of a reasonably long walk. But the smallest pups of all, Pongo's own family—how were they to walk over seventy miles? Lucky, Patch, Roly Poly, and the other boys struggled along bravely, but the girls stumbled and panted and had to have many rests. As for the Cadpig, she would never have reached the farm at all if the Sheepdog had not given her a lift. He lay down, and she climbed onto his back and held on to his long hair with her teeth. Even so, she nearly slipped off twice.

"She could never stay on our smooth backs," said Missis to Pongo. "If only I could wheel her in a doll's perambulator!"

"You couldn't walk to London on your hind legs," said Pongo, "even if we *had* a peramabulator."

At last they reached the big barn at the back of the farm where the Colonel lived. The tired pups snuggled into the hay and straw and instantly fell asleep. Pongo, Missis, and the Colonel stood at the door, trying to make plans.

The Colonel said, "I can't keep you here long. You would be found—besides, I couldn't feed so many. We must get you to London by easy stages, just a few miles a day."

"But where shall we sleep? Where shall we find food?" said Pongo anxiously.

"It will need *tremendous* organization," said the Colonel. "I hope to arrange the first stage at once, by Midnight Barking. I must bark some distance from the farm, or I shall wake my pets."

Pongo offered to bark with him, but the Sheepdog would not hear of it. "You two must rest. It's now nearly ten o'oclock. If my plan goes well I shall wake you at four, when there will still be over three hours of darkness. That will be long enough to get you to the place I have in mind."

"But my smallest daughter is so weak," said Missis. "How can she make *any* journey?"

The Colonel smiled—not that anyone could see that. "I have a plan for the little lass," he said. "Now, sleep, sleep, both of you."

So Pongo and Missis went into the dark barn and sniffed out their own family. Only Lucky stirred; he said he was trying to sleep with one eye open, so as to be on guard.

"You close *both* eyes," said Missis firmly.

And Lucky did, quite happy now his parents were there to take charge.

"What would happen if we *were* found here?" asked Missis. "Surely the people at the farm are kind? They wouldn't hurt us."

Pongo had been thinking about this. He guessed that as there had been so much in the papers about himself and Missis and their family, they might all get safely returned to the Dearlys. But the other puppies, what would happen to them? Even the dear, kind Dearlys would not take in eighty-two puppies they did not know. The poor things would be sent to a police station—anything might happen to them. But if once the Dearlys *saw* them, then all the puppies would suddenly belong to the Dearlys—just as they had suddenly seemed to belong to him, in the dark kitchen. Somehow, somehow he must get them all to London.

Missis felt just the same, but she did not see how the Cadpig and some of her sisters would make the journey.

"Well, sleep now," said Pongo, giving her a loving lick. "Are you glad you didn't, after all, have to bite a human?"

"The Badduns are no more human than Cruella is," said Missis. "Still, I'm glad I didn't have to soil my teeth."

They would not have fallen asleep so easily if they had known what the Sheepdog had just seen. Across the heath, lanterns were moving. The Badduns were out, searching for the missing puppies.

123

The Little Blue Cart

Pongo was dreaming he was back in Regent's Park, running after a stick thrown by Mr. Dearly, when a light tap on his shoulder woke him. It was Lieutenant Willow.

"The Colonel's compliments, and would you and your lady please come to him?"

Missis was sleeping peacefully. Pongo woke her gently, wondering what dream she would be leaving and if the dark barn would look as strange to her as it had to him a moment earlier. She sprang up at once, dazed and anxious.

"All well," said the cat soothingly. "Food and shelter are arranged for two days ahead. Reception for the Midnight Barking was excellent. Please follow me now."

She made no mention of the Baddun brothers with their lanterns, searching the heath.

It was still quite dark as they left the barn and crossed the farmyard. The cat led them to the back door of a large white farmhouse.

"Help me to push the door," she said. "The Colonel has unbolted it."

The door opened easily. They went through a kitchen and along a passage, at the end of which was an open door and a glimmer of light. The cat led them through the doorway, and they found themselves in a nursery lit by a night-light. At the far end, the Sheepdog stood beside a little painted bed in which was a very wide-awake two-year-old boy.

"This is my pet, Tommy," said the Colonel. "He very much wants to meet you."

Pongo and Missis went to the little boy, and he patted them both. Then he made some odd chuckling noises. They did not sound like Human nor did they sound like Dog. But the Sheepdog seemed to understand them, and Tommy seemed to understand what the Sheepdog answered. Pongo decided this was quite a new language, half Dog, half Human.

"Tommy wishes to lend you something," said the Colonel. "He knows how much you need it and is most anxious to help you. See, here it is."

Pongo and Missis then saw a little wooden cart, painted blue. It was made like a real farm cart, with four high wheels and a wooden railing all round it to keep the hay in—it was full of hay now. At the front was a long piece of wood with a wide crossbar at the end of it, so that Tommy could drag the cart about.

125

"You can choose two pups exactly the right size," said the Colonel, "and they can use the long piece of wood as a shaft—in between them—and take the crossbar in their mouths. Then they can pull the cart forward. And, if needed, pups at the back can push with their noses. Your smallest daughter can travel comfortably in the hay, and any puppy who is tired can sit beside her and take a rest."

Pongo and Missis examined the pretty cart delightedly. They were too big to get between it and the crossbar themselves, but they felt sure plenty of the bigger pups would fit.

"But does he really want us to take it?" asked Missis.

The Sheepdog then spoke to Tommy, who nodded his head again and again, while talking his extraordinary language.

His name and address are painted on the side," said the Sheepdog, "and he would be glad if it can be returned one day. But if that isn't possible, he will quite understand."

"If we ever get home, I feel sure Mr. Dearly will return it," said Pongo. "Please tell Tommy how very grateful we are."

The Sheepdog translated this to Tommy, who smiled more than ever and made more chuckling noises.

"He says he is pleased you are pleased, and would like to see all the puppies. I think it would be safe to march them all past his window when you leave—which should be soon now."

So they said good-bye to Tommy, and then the Sheepdog, going backwards, pulled the cart along the passage and out through the back door. He had quite a job.

"It's lucky my little pet sleeps on the ground floor," he said. "It's because our stairs are so steep. I could never have got this cart down them."

126

They went back to the barn and woke the pups, and all the bigger ones came outside and tried the cart on for size. (The moon was lower now but still gave plenty of light.) One family of eight fitted perfectly, and a dozen other pups could manage quite well, so Pongo arranged that all these should travel close to the cart and take it in turns to pull it, two at a time. The Cadpig was enchanted and settled down in the hay so that pups could practise pulling.

While this was happening, Pongo was told the plans made by Midnight Barking. Only five miles was to be travelled before dawn—which would not be for over three hours—to a village where a friend of the Colonel's lived at a bakery.

"And next door is a butcher's, so food will be all right," said the Colonel. "Then you'll do another five miles as soon as it's dark tomorrow—but my friend will tell you all about that. I hope to get you to London in ten or twelve days, billeting you where you can be safely hidden and fed. The last stages of the march will be the most difficult, but there are warehouses, if we can get in touch with their watchdogs. There's a Great Dane somewhere near Hampstead working on that already. Fine fellow. I hear he's a Brigadier-General."

Ten days or even longer! Missis felt her heart sink.

"Pongo," she said suddenly, "When is Christmas Day?"

"The day after tomorrow," said the Colonel. "No, bless me, it's *tomorrow*—because it's Christmas Eve already, even if it isn't light yet. Don't worry, Mrs. Pongo. You shall have some Christmas dinner."

But it was not food Missis was thinking about, but the Dearlys, all alone for Chrsitmas. Sometimes she forgot them for an hour or two, but never for very long. She thought now

127

of that last evening, when she had rested her head on Mrs. Dearly's knee, trying to make her understand—and of the warm white drawing room, where there was to have been a Christmas tree, with presents for the three dogs and the fifteen pups. Missis had heard the Dearlys planning it.

Pongo guessed his wife's thoughts—which was easy to do because his own were much the same. "Never mind, Missis," he said. "We'll be home by *next* Christmas."

The pups who were to take turns at pulling the little blue cart were now quite good at it.

"Then off you go," said the Colonel. "But first, our cows have asked you in to have a drink with them."

He led Pongo, Missis, and all the pups into the dim cowshed, where the hay still smelled of summer weather. The head cows, Blossom and Clover, were waiting to welcome them and tell them how to drink at the milk bar. The pups found this easy, especially those who could remember being fed by their mothers—though the smaller pups had to stand on their hind legs and be supported by other pups. The long, warm drink of milk made a splendid breakfast.

At last, after all their kind hostesses had been thanked, it was time to start.

Tommy stood at his window, peering into the moonlight, watching the march-past. Pongo and Missis wrinkled their noses at him in their best smile; every pup turned its head—except the Cadpig, who lay on her back in the hay-filled cart and waved all her four paws.

Pongo said to Missis, "How different Tommy is from the bad little boy who threw a stone at us."

Missis said, "The bad little boy was only bad because he

had never known dogs." And she was probably right.

The Colonel took them to the crossroads and started them on their way.

"I wish I could come with you, but I've a job to do," he said. Then he and the cat, who was riding on his back, said good-bye hastily and went off so fast that Pongo had to bark his thanks after them. The Colonel barked back that Sergeant-Major Lucky could now be a Lieutenant, then galloped away. Pongo stared in astonishment, wondering what job had to be done in such a hurry. It was a long time before he learned the truth.

The Colonel had just been informed by Lieutenant Willow that the Baddun brothers, having failed to find the puppies on the heath, were now on the outskirts of the village, less than half a mile behind the Dalmatians. He could think of only one thing to do, and he set out to do it—with great pleasure.

He galloped until he saw the Badduns' lanterns ahead of him. Then he told the cat to get off his back. The minute she was off, he hurled himself at the Badduns and bit both brothers in both legs. Seldom can four legs have been bitten so fast by one dog. The Badduns howled with rage, fear, and pain, dropped their lanterns, and limped back to Hell Hall as quickly as possible. (It is difficult to limp well when you are lame in both legs.) They never knew what bit them. They only knew it bit hard.

"Good work, Colonel," said Lieutenant Willow.

"I'm promoting you to Captain," said the Sheepdog. Then he gave a modest little cough and added, "Oh, by the way! I've just made myself a Brigadier-General."

130

Christmas Eve

MEANWHILE, the Dalmatian army was swinging along the road in fine style. Though cold, the night was very still. The pups were rested and hopeful. And the fact that a tired little dog could take a rest with the Cadpig in her cart made tired little dogs feel less tired. Indeed, Missis at first had to insist that the smaller pups take turns to rest. But progress was not really fast. There were so many pauses while the pups who pulled the cart were changed, pauses while pups got in and out of the cart; and every half-mile the whole army had a rest. Still, all went wonderfully well until they were within half a mile of the village where they were to spend the day.

There was a hint of dawn in the sky now, but Pongo felt

sure they could reach the village before it was dangerously light. He quickened the pace slightly and told the pups to think of breakfast ahead of them at the bakery.

It was soon after this that the Cadpig called out, "Look! Little painted houses on wheels"

Pongo saw them at the same moment, and he knew they were not houses. They were caravans.

He had seen them once when out with Mr. Dearly and had heard Mr. Dearly say that gipsies lived in caravans and gipsies sometimes stole valuable dogs.

"Halt!" said Pongo instantly.

Could they get past the caravans without being seen? He wasn't going to risk it. Between them and the nearest caravan was an open gate. He would lead the puppies through it and take them through the fields until they were well past the caravans. Swiftly he gave his instructions, which were handed on from pup to pup: "We are to keep dead quiet and follow Pongo through the gate."

And thus did the owner of one of the keenest brains in Dogdom make one of his few mistakes. For in the caravan nearest to them an old gipsy woman was awake and looking out of the little back window. She saw the approaching Dalmatians and at once woke her husband. He was beside her at the window just as Pongo led the way into the field.

The old gipsy woman never read newspapers, so she knew nothing about the stolen puppies. But she knew that here were many valuable dogs. And she knew something else, which Pongo did not know. There is a connection between Dalmations and gipsies. Many people believe that it was the gipsies who first brought Dalmatians to England, long, long ago. And

132

nothing like as long ago as that, there were gipsies who travelled round England with Dalmatians trained to do tricks. And these performing dogs earned money for the gipsies. The old woman could remember such dogs, and she thought how splendid it would be if all these Dalmatians could be trained as money-earners.

"Quick! Close the gate!" she said to her husband. She spoke in the strange gipsy language, which is called Romany. "The only other way out of that field is through a break in the hedge. I will rouse the camp, and we will all stop the dogs there and catch them."

In less that two minutes the whole gipsy encampment was awake. Children cried, dogs barked, horses neighed. It was still so dark that it took Pongo five minutes to find the break in the hedge. And when he found it, he also found the way barred. All the gipsies were there, with sticks and ropes.

"Back to the gate, as fast as you can!" he cried to the pups.

But when they reached the gate it was closed. They were trapped.

Pongo barked loudly, hoping that some gipsy dog might help him. Many gipsy dogs barked in answer, but they had all been shut up in the caravans in case they should fight the Dalmatians. In any case, they barked only in Romany, so they could not understand a word Pongo said.

But someone else did. Suddenly Pongo heard the high neigh of a horse close at hand—and, oh, most wonderful, the horse could neigh normally, as well as in Romany. It understood Pongo, and he understood it. Horses are nearly always friendly to Dalmatians—perhaps because of those days when Dalmatians were trained to follow carriages. This horse was not

133

old enough to remember such days, but he took an instant liking to Pongo, Missis, and all the pups. If these pleasant creatures wished to come out of the field, nothing could be easier. He strolled up, opened the gate with his long, strong teeth, and swung it back. Out poured the puppies.

"Lead them past the caravans as fast as you can!" Pongo shouted to Missis, and waited to see the last pup out of the field.

"What a *very* large family you and your wife have," said the horse. "My wife and I have never had more than the one. Well, good luck to you."

He waved aside Pongo's thanks and then, being a very tidy horse, he carefully closed the gate again. So never did the gipsies—all waiting at the break in the hedge—know how their prisoners got away.

Helter-skelter along the road went Missis, the puppies, and, finally, Pongo. The pups who drew the Cadpig's cart stuck faithfully to their task.) The shut-in Romany dogs heard them and shook the caravans in their efforts to get out. Volleys of furious barking came from the little windows.

"The caravans bark but the dogs move on," remarked Pongo when he felt they were out of danger.

A few minutes later they reached the village where they were to sleep. The Sheepdog's friend, a handsome Collie, was waiting to welcome them.

"No talk until you're safely hidden," he said. "It's almost light."

Quickly they followed him across the village green to three old gabled houses. The baker's was in the middle, between the butcher's and the chimney-sweep's. The baker and the

134

butcher and the sweep were all widowers and, as it was Sunday, had already gone to spend Christmas with their married daughters, which was just as well.

The baker's shop would not have been nearly big enough to house all the pups, but luckily there was a large bakehouse at the back. And soon every pup was safely in and enjoying a splendid sausage roll. Pongo and Missis chatted to the Collie while they ate. He shook his head worriedly when he heard about the gipsies.

"A narrow escape," he said. "The trouble is that Dalmatians are such noticeable dogs. Ninety-nine of you together are spectacular—though I mean it as a compliment. You'd be much safer if you were black."

"Like that nice little pup over there," said Missis.

"What pup?" The Collie looked across the bakehouse, then said sharply, "That pup doesn't belong in this village. Who are you, my lad? Where have you come from?"

The black pup did not answer. Instead, he came running to Missis and butted her in the stomach.

"Here, hold hard, young man!" said Missis. Then she gasped. "Goodness, it is! It isn't! It *is* Roly Poly!"

The fat puppy who was always getting into mischief had found his way into a shed at the back of the sweep's house and had a fight with a bag of soot.

"Mercy, you'll need some washing!" said his mother.

Then it was that one of the keenest brains in Dogdom had one of its brainiest waves.

"Roly Poly," said Pongo, "was there a lot of soot at the sweep's?"

"Bags and bags," said Roly Poly.

135

"Then we are *all* going to be black dogs," said Pongo.

"Your husband is a genius," said the Collie to Missis as he showed them all into the sweep's shed.

There was any amount of soot—waiting to have done with it whatever sweeps do do with soot.

"Ten dogs forward at a time!" commanded Pongo. "Pups roll! Pups rub noses!"

In a very short time there were ninety-seven pitchblack pups.

"And now, my love," said Pongo to Missis. Let *us* take a roll in the soot."

Frankly, Missis did not fancy it. She hated soiling her gleaming white hair and losing its smart contrast with her beautiful black spots. But when Pongo had helped her with the final touches he said: "Why, Missis, as a black dog, you're slimmer than ever. You're positively *svelte!*" and then she felt much better.

Then Pongo said, "How does soot suit me?"

"Suit soots you beautifully," said Missis, and all the pups roared with laughter at her mistake.

Then they all went back to the bakehouse and settled down to sleep. The Collie said he would call them as soon as it was dark. They would have only five miles to go—to another bakery—but he felt they should get the journey over early as he had heard there might be snow.

"But there may be cars on the road until late, as it is Christmas Eve—and Sunday," he told them. "So you must go by the fields. I shall escort you. Rest well now."

Poor Missis! When she awoke in the late afternoon and looked around her, she dissolved into sooty tears.

"I can't tell one pup from the other now they're black," she moaned. But she soon found she could, though she could never have explained how she managed it.

Another meal had been organized, but it was not all that could have been wished, because the butcher had meanly locked up his shop.

"This clears the bakery out," said the Collie, carrying in the last stale loaf. "But there will be a good supper waiting for you. And the journey oughtn't to take more than three or four hours." He then went off to see if there was any news coming in by the Twilight Barking.

After half an hour or so, Pongo began to feel anxious. It was quite dark now; they ought to be off. What was delaying the Collie?

"Listen!" said Missis suddenly.

Very, very faintly, they could hear the Collie barking. He was calling Pongo's name, again and again.

Pongo and Missis ran out of the bakehouse to the little yard at the back. Now they could hear the Collie more clearly. But he was obviously some way off. Pongo barked in answer to him. Then swiftly the Collie told them what had happened.

He was locked in a house across the green, with no hope of getting out. The postmistress had promised to look after him while the baker was away for Christmas. She had decided it was too cold a night for a dog to be out, hauled him in, and gone out for the evening. He had tried every door and every window but could undo none of them. It was impossible for him to escort the Dalmatians, as he had promised.

"But you *can't* miss your way, Pongo," he barked. "Out over the field at the back of the bakehouse and *straight* on for five miles."

137

Pongo told him not to worry. But the poor Collie was most unhappy. "Here I am, locked in with a warm fire and a good supper—and powerless to help you."

Both Pongo and Missis told him to eat the supper and enjoy the fire, and thanked him for all he had done.

"And now, off we go," said Pongo, bringing the pups out of the bakehouse. "And no straggling! Because it would be very easy to lose a black pup on a dark night."

But it was not really a very dark night, for already the moon was rising and the stars were out. There was one specially large, bright star.

"The Collie said straight ahead, and that star is straight ahead," said Pongo. "So we'll steer by it." He was thankful they were going by way of the fields and not by the road— for he remembered that Cruella had told the Baddun brothers she would come down "tomorrow night" to count the bodies. Now it *was* "tomorrow night" and the great zebra-striped car would be somewhere on the road from London to Suffolk. How terrible it would be to meet it! He imagined the glare from the headlights, imagined Cruella driving straight at the army of panic-stricken puppies. Yes, he would certainly avoid the roads! But, even so, it was frightening to know that Cruella might be quite near. He put the thought from his mind as he and Missis got the pups into marching order.

Their way lay through grassy meadows over which the Cadpig's cart trundled smoothly. At every hedge and ditch Pongo paused and counted the pups to see none had strayed, and Missis changed the pups who drew the cart and the pups who rested in it. Already even the smallest puppies were getting hardier—even the Cadpig got out of the cart and walked three fields before getting in again.

"Soon we shall be able to do ten miles a day," said Pongo.

They had travelled about three miles when the first disaster of the night happened. There was a sudden bump, and a wild squeal from the Cadpig. A wheel had come off the little blue cart.

Pongo saw at once that the cart could be mended. A wooden peg which fixed the hub of the wheel to the axle had come out. But could he ever, using his teeth, put this peg back? He tried—and failed.

"Could the Cadpig manage without the cart?" he whispered to Missis.

Missis shook her head. Walking three fields had been enough for her smallest daughter. And her other daughters could not walk more than a mile without a rest.

"Then mend the cart I must," said Pongo. "And you must help me, by holding the wheel in position."

They tried and tried, without success. Then, while they were resting for a moment, Missis noticed that many of the pups were shivering.

"They'd better keep warm by running races," said Pongo.

"But that would tire them," said Missis. "Couldn't they all go to that barn over there?"

They could just see a big tiled roof, two short fields away— not very clearly, because the moon was behind clouds; it was this lack of light which made it so hard to mend the cart.

"That's a good idea," said Pongo. "And when the cart's mended, we can bring it along and call for them all."

Missis said the Cadpig had better stay in the cart and keep warm in the hay, but the Cadpig wanted to go with the others and see the barn—she felt sure she could walk two short fields. So Missis let her go. Two strong pups the right size to draw the cart stayed behind. They said they did not mind the cold.

So ninety-five pups, led by Lieutenant Lucky, set off briskly for the barn. But when they got there it did not look at all like the barn at the Sheepdog's farm. It was built of grey stone and had long windows, some with coloured glass in them, and at one end was a tower.

"Why, there's a Folly!" said the Cadpig, remembering the tower of the Folly at Hell Hall.

Lucky was looking for a door, but when he found one it was firmly shut. He told the pups to wait for him while he went round the building looking for some other way in.

The Cadpig did not wait. "Come on," she said to her devoted brother Patch. "I want to look at that Folly."

And when they got to the tower they saw a narrow door that was not quite closed. It was too heavy for them to push, but they could —just—just—squeeze through.

Inside, this tower was nothing like the one at Hell Hall. And it opened into the grey stone building.

"No hay in this barn," said the Cadpig.

She had counted on the hay for warmth, but she soon found she was warm enough without it, for there was a big stove alight. It had a long iron pipe for a chimney, which went right up through the raftered ceiling. The moon was out again now, and its light was streaming in through the tall windows, so that the clear glass made silver patterns on the stone floor and the coloured glass made blue, gold, and rose patterns. The

Cadpig patted one of the coloured patterns with a delicate paw.

"I love this barn," she said.

Patch said, "I don't think it *is* a barn." But he liked it as much as the Cadpig did.

They wandered around—and suddenly they made a discovery. Whatever this mysterious place was, it was certainly intended for puppies. For in front of every seat—and there were many seats—was a puppy-sized dog-bed, padded and most comfortable.

"Why, it's just *meant* for us all to sleep in!" said the Cadpig.

"I'll tell the other pups," said Patch, starting for the door. A glad cry from the Cadpig called him back.

"Look, look! Television!"

But it was not like the television at Hell Hall. It was much larger. And the figures on the screen did not move or speak. Indeed, it was not a screen. The figures were really there, on a low platform, humans and animals, most lifelike, though smaller than in real life. They were in a stable, above which was one bright star.

"Look at the little humans, kneeling," said Patch.

"And there's a kind of a cow," said the Cadpig, remembering the cows at the farm, who had given all the pups milk.

"And a kind of a horse," said Patch, remembering the helpful horse who had let them all out of the field.

"No dogs," said the Cadpig. "What a pity! But I like it much better than ordinary television. Only I don't know why."

Then they heard Lucky and the others, who had found their way in. Soon every pup was lying curled up on a comfortable dog-bed and fast asleep—except the Cadpig. She had dragged along one of the dog-beds by its most convenient little carpet ear, and was sitting on it, wide awake, gazing and gazing at this new and far more beautiful television.

Once the moon came out from behind the clouds Pongo managed to mend the wheel—oh, the feeling of satisfaction when the peg slipped into place! Missis too felt proud. Had she not *held* the wheel? She, a dog who had never understood machinery! Quickly the two waiting pups seized the crossbar in their mouths. Then off they all went to the barn.

But as they drew nearer, Pongo saw this was no barn.

"Surely they can't have gone in *there?*" he said to Missis.

"Why not, if they were cold?" said Missis. "And they are far too young to know they would not be welcome."

Pongo and Missis both knew that humans did not like dogs to go into buildings which had towers and tall, narrow windows. They had no idea why, and had at first been a little hurt when told firmly to wait outside. But Mrs. Dearly had once said, "We would love you to come in if it was allowed. And *I* would go in far oftener if *you* could." So it was obviously one of those mysterious things such as no one—not even humans—ever being allowed to walk on certain parts of the grass in Regent's Park.

"We must get them out quickly," said Pongo, "and go on with our journey."

They soon found the door in the tower—which the biggest pups had pushed wide open. Because Missis had always been left outside, she disliked these curious buildings with towers and high windows; but the minute she got inside she changed her mind. This was a wonderful place—so peaceful and, somehow, so welcoming.

"But where are the pups?" she said, peering all around.

She saw lots of black patches on the moonlit floor but had quite forgotten that all the pups were now black. Then she remembered and as she drew nearer to the sleeping pups, tears sprang to her eyes.

"Look, look at all the puppy-beds!" she cried. "What *good* people must live here!"

"It can't be the kind of place I thought it was," said Pongo.

He was about to wake the puppies when Missis stopped him. "Let me sit by the stove for a little while," she said.

"Not too long, my dear," said Pongo.

He need not have worried. Missis sat still for only a few minutes. Then she got up, shook herself, and said brightly, "Let us start now. Things are going to be all right."

An hour or so later, just before the evening service, the Verger said to the Vicar, "I think there must be something wrong with the stove, sir."

On every hassock he had found a small circular patch of soot.

Miracle Needed

LAST lap before supper," said Pongo as they started off again across the moonlit fields.

It was the most cheering thing he could have said, for the ninety-seven puppies were now extremely hungry. He had guessed this because he was hungry himself. And so was Missis. But she was feeling too peaceful to mind.

They went on for nearly two miles; then Pongo saw a long row of cottage roofs ahead across the fields.

"This should be it," he said.

What is that glow in the sky beyond the roof-tops?" asked Missis.

Pongo was puzzled. He had seen such a glow in the sky

144

over towns which had many lights, but never over a village.
And this was a very bright glow. "Perhaps it's a larger place
than we expected it to be," he said, and did not feel it would
be safe to go any nearer until some dog came to meet them.
He called a halt and barked news of their arrival.

He was answered at once, by a bark that said, "Wait where
you are. I am coming." And though he did not tell Missis,
Pongo felt there was something odd about this bark that answered his. For one thing, there were no cheerful words of
welcome.

Soon a graceful red Setter came dashing towards them. They
guessed, even before she spoke, that something was very
wrong.

"The bakery's on fire!" she gasped.

The blaze, due to a faulty chimney, had begun only a
few minutes before—the fire engine had not yet arrived. No
one had been hurt, but the bakehouse was full of flames
and smoke—all the food spread out for the Dalmatians was
burned.

"There's nothing for you to eat and nowhere for you to
sleep," moaned the poor Setter—she was hysterical. "And the
village street's full of people." She looked pitifully at Missis.
"All your poor hungry puppies!"

The strange thing was that Missis felt quite calm. She tried
to comfort the Setter, saying they would go to some barn.

"But no arrangements are made," wailed the Setter. "And
there's no spare food anywhere. All the village dogs brought
what they could to the bakery."

Just then came a shrill whistle.

"My pet is calling me," said the Setter. "He's the doctor

145

here. There's no dog at the bakery, so I was chosen to arrange everything—because I took first prize in a dog show. And now I've failed you."

"You have *not* failed," said Missis. "No one could say the fire was act of dog. Go back to your pet and don't worry. We shall simply go on to the next village."

Really?" said the Setter, gasping again—but with relief.

Missis kissed her on the nose. "Off with you, my dear, and don't give the matter another thought. And thank you for all you did."

The whistle came again, and the Setter ran off, wildly waving her feathered tail.

"Feather-brained as well as feather-tailed," said Pongo.

"Just very young," said Missis gently. "I doubt if she's had a family yet. Well, on to the next village."

"Thank you for being so brave, dear Missis," said Pongo. "But where *is* the next village?"

"In the country there are villages in *every* direction," said Missis brightly.

Desperately worried though he was, Pongo smiled lovingly at her. Then he said, "We will go to the road now."

"But what about traffic, Pongo?"

"We shall not be very long on the road," said Pongo.

Then he told her what he had decided. Even if the next village should only be a few miles away, many of the pups were too tired and too hungry to get there—some of them were already asleep on the frozen ground. And every minute it got colder.

"And even if we could get to the next village, where should we sleep. Missis, what should we eat, with no plans made

146

ahead? We must give in, my dear. Come, wake the pups! Quick march, everyone!"

The waking pups whimpered and shivered, and Missis saw that even the strongest pups were now wretchedly cold. So she helped Pongo to make them all march briskly.

Then she whispered, "But *how* do we give in, Pongo?"

Pongo said, "We must go into the village and find the police station."

Missis stared at him in horror. "No, Pongo, no! The police will take the puppies from us!"

"But they will feed them, Missis. And perhaps we shall be kept together until Mr. Dearly has been told about us. They will have read the papers. They will know we are the Missing Dalmatians."

"But we are not Dalmatians any more, Pongo," cried Missis. "We are black. They will think we are ordinary stray dogs. And we are illegal—ninety-nine dogs without collars. We shall be put in prison."

"No, Missis!" But Pongo was shaken. He had forgotten they were now black dogs. Suppose the police did *not* recognize them? Suppose the Dearlys were never told about them? What happened to stray dogs that no one claimed?

"Please, Pongo, I beg you!" cried Missis. "Let us go on with our journey! I *know* it will be all right."

They had now reached the road and were on the edge of the village. Pongo was faced with a terrible choice. But it still seemed to him wiser to trust the police than to lead the hungry, exhuasted puppies into the bitter winter night.

"Missis, dear Missis, we *must* go to the police station," he said, and turned towards the village. They could now see the

147

burning bakery, and at that moment a huge flame leaped up through the roof. By its light Pongo saw the whole village street, with the villagers making a human chain to hand along buckets of water. And he also saw something else—something which made him stop dead, shouting, "Halt!" at the top of his bark.

In front of the burning bakery was a great striped black-and white car. And with it was Cruella de Vil—standing right up on the roof of the car, where she had climbed so as to get a good view of the fire. Her white face and absolutely simple white mink cloak no longer looked white. From head to foot she was bathed in the red-gold flicker of the flames. And as they leaped higher and higher she clapped her hands in delight.

The next instant there was a wild clamour of bells as the fire engine arrived at last. The noise, the flames, and, above all, the sight of Cruella were too much for many of the puppies. Squealing in terror, they turned and fled, with Pongo, Missis, and Lucky desperately trying to call them to order.

Fortunately, the clamour from the fire engine prevented anyone in the village from hearing the barking and yapping. And after a little while the terrified pups obeyed Pongo's orders and stopped their headlong flight. They were very shamefaced as Pongo told them that, though he quite understood how they had felt, they must never, never behave in such a panic-stricken way and must always, always obey orders instantly. Then he praised the pups who had stuck to the Cadpig's cart, praised Patch for staying close to the Cadpig, rescued Roly Poly from a ditch, and counted the pups carefully. He did all this as hurriedly as possible, for he knew now that they must

148

press on with their journey. There was no way they could get to the police station without passing Cruella de Vil.

Their plight was now worse than ever. They not only had to face the dangers of hunger and cold, there was the added danger of Cruella. They knew from the direction her car was facing that their enemy must have already been to Hell Hall and learned that they had escaped, and must now be on her way back to London. At any moment she might leave the fire and overtake them.

If only they could have left the road and travelled by the fields again! But there were now woods on either side of the road, woods so thick that the army could not have kept together.

"But we can hide in there, if we see the car's headlights," said Pongo, and explained this to the puppies. Then the army was on the march again.

"At least the pups are warm now," said Missis. "And they have forgotten how tired and hungry they are. It will be all right, Pongo."

The pace was certainly good for a couple of miles; then it got slower and slower.

"The puppies will have to rest," said Missis. "And this is a good place for it."

There was now a wide, grassy verge to the road. The moment Pongo called a halt, the pups sank down on the frosty grass. Many of them at once fell asleep.

"They ought not to sleep," said Pongo anxiously.

"Let them, for a little while," said Missis.

The Cadpig was not asleep. She sat up in her cart and said, "Will there be a barn soon, with kind cows and warm milk?"

149

"I'm sure there will be *something* nice," said Missis. "Snuggle down in your hay, my darling. Pongo, how strangely quiet it is."

They could no longer hear any sounds from the village. No breath of wind rustled the grass or stirred the trees. The world seemed frozen into a silvery, silent stillness.

Something soft and fluffy touched Pongo's head, something that puzzled him. Then, as he realized what it was, Missis whispered, "Look, Pongo! Look at the puppies!"

Tiny white dots were appearing on the sooty black coats. Snow had begun to fall.

Missis said, smiling, "Instead of being white pups with black spots they are turning into black pups with white spots—only soon they will be all white. How soft and gentle the snow is!"

Pongo was not smiling. He cried, "If they sleep on until it has covered them, they will never wake—they will freeze to death beneath that soft, gentle snow! Wake up, pups! Wake up!"

By now, every pup but Lucky and the Cadpig had fallen into a deep, exhausted sleep. Lucky helped his parents to rouse them, and the Cadpig helped too, sitting up in her cart and yapping piercingly. The poor pups begged to be left to sleep, and those who tottered onto their feet soon tottered off them again.

"We shall never get them going," said Pongo despairingly.

For a moment the Cadpig stopped yapping, and there was a sudden silence. Then, from the village behind them, came the strident blare of the loudest motor-horn in England.

The pups sprang up, their exhaustion driven away by terror.

"To the woods!" cried Pongo. Then he saw that the woods

were now protected by wire netting, through which not even the smallest pup could squeeze. And there was no ditch to hide in. But he could see that the woods ended, not very far ahead. "We must go on," he cried. "There may be fields, there may be a ditch."

The horn sounded again, repeatedly. Pongo guessed that the fire engine had put out the fire, and now Cruella was scattering the villagers as she drove on her way. Already she would be less than two miles behind them—and the great striped car could travel two miles in less than two minutes. But the woods were ending, there were fields ahead!

"To the fields!" cried Pongo. "Faster, faster!"

The pups made a great spurt forward, then fell back in dismay. For though the woods ended, the wire netting still continued, on both sides of them. There was still no way off the road. And the horn sounded again—louder and nearer.

"Nothing but a miracle can save us now," said Pongo.

"Then we must find a miracle," said Missis firmly. "Pongo, what *is* a miracle?"

It was at that moment that they suddenly saw, through the swirling snow, a very large van drawn up on the road ahead of them. The tailboard was down, and the inside of the van was lit by electric light. And sitting there, on a newspaper, was a Staffordshire Terrier with a short clay pipe in his mouth. That is, it looked like a clay pipe. It was really made of sugar and had once had a fine long stem. Now the Staffordshire drew the bowl of the pipe into his mouth and ate it. Then he looked up from the newspaper—which he was reading as well as sitting on—and stared in astonishment at the army of pups rushing helter-skelter towards him.

151

"Help, help, help!" barked Pongo. "We are being pursued. How soon can we get off this road?"

"I don't know, mate," barked back the Staffordshire. "You'd better hide in my van."

"The miracle, the miracle!" gasped Pongo to Missis.

"Quickly, pups! Jump into the nice miracle," said Missis, who now thought "miracle" was another name for a removal van.

A swarm of pups surged up the tailboard. Up went the Cadpig's cart, pulled from the front and pushed from behind. Then more and more pups jumped or scrambled up until the entire army was in.

Golly, there are a lot of you," said the Staffordshire, who had flattened himself against the side of the van. "Lucky the van was empty. Who's after you, mates? Old Nick?"

"Some relation of his, I think," said Pongo. The strident horn sounded again, and now two strong headlights could be seen in the distance. "And she's in that car."

"Then I'd better put the light off," said the Staffordshire, neatly working the switch with his teeth. "That's better."

Pongo's heart seemed to miss a beat. Suddenly he knew that letting the pups get into the van had been a terrible mistake.

"But the car's headlights will shine in," he gasped. "Our enemy will see the pups."

"Not black pups in a black van," said the Staffordshire. "Not if they close their eyes."

Oh, excellent suggestion! Quickly Pongo gave the command.

"Pups, close your eyes—or they will reflect the car's head-

152

lights and shine like jewels in the darkness. Close them and do not open them, however frightened you are, until I give the word. Remember, your lives may depend on your obedience now. Close your eyes and keep them closed!"

Instantly all the puppies closed their eyes tight. And now the car's headlights were less than a quarter of a mile away.

"Close your eyes, Missis," said Pongo.

"And don't forget to close your own, mate," said the Staffordshire.

Now the car's powerful engine could be heard. The strident horn blared again and again, as if telling the van to get out of the way. Louder and louder grew the noise from the engine. The glare from the headlights was now so intense that Pongo was conscious of it through his tightly shut eyelids. Would the pups obey orders? Or would terror make them look towards the oncoming car? Pongo himself had a wild desire to do so and a wild fear that the car was going to crash into the van. The noise of horn and engine grew deafening; the glare seemed blinding, even to closed eyes. Then, with a roar, the great striped car was on them—and past them, roaring on and on into the night!

"You may open your eyes now, my brave, obedient pups," cried Pongo. And indeed they deserved praise, for not one eye had been opened.

"That was quite a car, mate," said the Staffordshire to Pongo. "You must have quite an enemy. Who are you, anyway? The local pack of soot-hounds?" Then he suddenly stared very hard at Pongo's nose. "Well, swelp me if it *isn't* soot! And it doesn't fool me. You're the Missing Dalmatians. Want a lift back to London?"

153

A lift? A lift all the way in this wonderful van! Pongo and Missis could hardly believe it. Swiftly the pups settled to sleep on the rugs and blankets used for wrapping furniture.

"But why are there so many pups?" said the Staffordshire. "The newspapers don't know the half of it, nor the quarter. They think there are only fifteen missing."

Pongo started to explain, but the Staffordshire said they would talk during the drive to London. "My pets will be out of that house there any minute. Fancy us doing a removal on a Sunday—*and* Christmas Eve. But the van broke down yesterday, and we had to finish the job."

"How many days will the journey to London take?" asked Missis.

Days?" said the Staffordshire. "It won't take much more than a couple of hours, if *I* know my pets. They want to get home to finish decorating their kids' Christmas trees. Sssh, now! Pipe down, both of you."

A large man in a rough apron was coming out of a nearby house. Missis thought, "As soon as one danger is past, another threatens." Would they all be turned out of the miracle?

The Staffordshire, wagging his tail enthusiastically, hurled himself at the man's chest, nearly knocking him down.

"Look out, Bill!" said the man, over his shoulder. "The Canine Cannon Ball's feeling frisky."

Bill was an even larger man, but even he was shaken by the Staffordshire's loving welcome.

"Get down, you Self-launched Bomb," he shouted with great affection.

The two men and the Staffordshire came back to the van, and the Staffordshire jumped inside. The sooty Dalmatians, huddled together, were invisible in the darkness.

Want to ride inside, do you" said Bill. "Well, it *is* cold." He put the tailboard up and shouted, "Next stop, St. John's Wood." A moment later the van started.

St. John's Wood! Surely, that was where the Splendid Vet lived—quite close to Regent's Park! What wonderful, wonderful luck, thought Pongo. Just then he heard a clock strike. It was still only eight o'clock.

Missis!" he cried. "We shall get home tonight! We shall be home for Christmas!"

Yes, Pongo," said Missis gaily. But she did not feel as gay as she sounded. For Missis, who had been so brave, so confident up to the moment they had found the miracle, had suddenly been smitten by a great fear. Suppose the Dearlys did not recognize them now they were black dogs? Suppose the dear, dear Dearlys turned them away?

She kept her fears to herself. Why should she frighten Pongo with them? How fast the miracle was travelling! She thought of the days it had taken her and Pongo to reach Suffolk on foot. Why, it seemed like weeks since they had left London! Yet it was only—how long? Could it be only *four* days? They'd slept one day in the stable at the inn, one day at the dear Spaniel's, one day in the Folly, part of a night in the barn after the escape from Hell Hall, then a day at the bakery. So much had happened in so short a time. And now, would it be all right when they got home? Would it? Would it?

Meanwhile, Pongo had his own worries. He had been telling the Staffordshire all about Cruella and had remembered what she had said that night at Hell Hall—how she intended to wait until people had forgotten about the stolen puppies, and then start her Dalmatian fur farm again. Surely he and Missis would get this lot of puppies safely home (it had never occurred to *him* that the Dearlys might not let them in), but what of the future? How could he make sure that other puppies did not end up as fur coats later on? He asked for advice.

"Why not kill this Cruella?" said the Staffordshire. "And I'll help you. Let's make a date for it now."

Pongo shook his head. He had come to believe that Cruella was not an ordinary human but some kind of devil. If so, could one kill her? In any case, he didn't want his pups to have a killer-dog for a father. He would have sprung at Cruella if she had attacked any pup, but he didn't fancy cold-blooded murder. He told the Staffordshire so.

"Your blood would soon warm up, once you started the job," said the Staffordshire. "Well, let me know if you change your mind. And now you take a nap, mate. You've still got quite a job ahead of you."

The Staffordshire, like Missis, wondered if the Dearlys would recognize these black Dalmatians—and if even the kindest pets would take in so many pups. But he said nothing of this to Pongo.

Missis, lulled by the movement of the van, had fallen asleep. Soon Pongo slept too. But their dreams were haunted by their separate anxieties.

On and on through the dark went the mile-eating miracle.

The White Cat's
Revenge

T HE Staffordshire woke them in good time—every pup must be ready to leap out of the van the minute the tailboard was put down.

"Not that my dear pets would hurt you if they saw you," said the Staffordshire. "But it might cause delay. The van will stop in a big, dark garage. Streak out, turn sharp left, and you will be in a dimly lit mews—and on your way. We'll say good-bye now."

"Can we send you news on the Twilight Barking?" asked Pongo.

"Hardly ever get the chance to listen to it," said the Staffordshire. "But I shall get news of you all right. I'm a great

157

one for newspapers—they pass the time on the road. Always plenty of them in the van; we use them for packing. Well, here we are."

The van stopped. The Staffordshire started to bark loudly.

"Let him out, Jim," said Bill. "Before he breaks the Sound Barrier."

Down came the tailboard. Out shot the Staffordshire. This time he managed to knock Jim right down, before turning to Bill, whom he tackled low.

"Just about winded me, he has," said Bill proudly. "Grrh, you Flying Saucer, you!"

Jim got to his feet and spoke lovingly to the Staffordshire. "If England had six of you, we shouldn't need no army," he said. "Come home and get your supper, you Misguided Missile."

Bill and Jim had been much too occupied to notice the black dogs streaming out of the van and out of the dark garage into the mews. Snow had been falling for hours, so that London was all white. The pups had scarcely noticed the snow while they were running away from Cruella's car. Now they at once fell in love with this beautiful feathery stuff—it raised their spirits wonderfully. And they felt well rested after their sleep in the van. They were still hungry, but they didn't mind that much because they were expecting a wonderful supper. Hearing them counting on this, poor Missis felt more anxious than ever.

Bill, Jim, and the Staffordshire had gone out of the garage by another way, so Pongo let the pups play in the snowy mews for a few minutes. Then Missis persuaded the Cadpig to get back into her cart, and off they went. Because of the snow

there were very few people about—which was just as well, as the army of black dogs was now very noticeable against the white streets. The only person who saw them was an elderly gentleman on his way to a late party. He rubbed his eyes, then shook his head and murmured, "And I haven't even *begun* Christmas yet."

It took only a few minutes to reach the Outer Circle. How beautiful Regent's Park looked, snowy under the stars!

Pongo said, Missis, do you remember what I told you when we said good-bye to the park?"

Missis answered, "You told me to think of the day when we would come back with fifeen puppies running behind us. And now we have ninety-seven."

They had not come back to the Outer Circle by the way they had left it, but were at the other side of the park, close to Cruella de Vil's house. As they drew near to it, Pongo saw that every window was dark, so he thought it would be safe to call a moment's halt.

"Look, pups," he told them. "That is our enemy's house."

Lucky said, "May we scratch it and bite it?"

"You would only hurt your nails and your teeth," said Pongo, looking up at the huge house.

Missis was looking down into the area. Something moved there—something only a little less white than the snow. It was Cruella's Persian cat.

Her back was arched, and she was spitting angrily. Pongo said quickly, "Madam, none of us would ever dream of hurting you."

The white cat said, "That's the civilest speech I ever had

from a dog. Who are you? There are no black dogs round here."

We are not usually black except for our spots," said Pongo. "We once visited your house—"

He got no further because the white cat guessed everything—as well she might, after all the talk she had heard between Mr. and Mrs. de Vil.

"And you've rescued all the pups from Hell Hall! Well, bravo, bravo! I couldn't be more pleased."

Then Missis remembered what Cruella de Vil had said on the night when the puppies were born, and she spoke to the white cat very kindly, saying, "I might have known you would sympathize—for I once heard you lost many kittens in early infancy."

"Forty-four, to the present date," said the white cat. "All drowned by the fiend I live with."

"Why don't you leave her?" asked Pongo.

"I bide my time," said the white cat. "I wait for my full revenge. I can't do much on my own—I've only two pairs of paws. But I scare the servants away—any cat can make a house seem haunted. I let the place become overrun with mice. And, oh, how I scratch the furniture! Though it's heartbreaking how little she notices it—she's such a rotten housewife. Why not let your pups come in and do some damage now?"

"Oh, please, please let us!" clamoured all the pups.

Pongo shook his head. "Cruella will be back. I'm surprised she's not home already."

"Oh, she's been back," said the white cat, "and gone out to dinner. She had to, because I scared another batch of

161

servants away this morning—as a little Christmas present for her. *Do* come in!"

"No, no, Pongo!" cried Missis. "This is no moment for revenge. We should get the pups home. They are hungry."

But the pups clamoured louder than ever. "Please, please, *please* let us damage Cruella's house!" They made so much noise that Missis could not hear what the white cat was now saying to Pongo. At last he turned, quietened the pups, and said, "Missis, I now feel that we *should* do as our friend here suggests. It would take me a long time to explain why, so will you trust me, please?"

"Of course, Pongo," said Missis loyally. "And if you're sure we really ought to be revenged on Cruella—well, naturally, I shall enjoy it."

"Then follow me," said the white cat. "There's a way in at the back."

Lucky and two big, loud-barked pups were left on guard. They were sorry to miss the fun, but duty was duty.

Three barks if you sight the striped car or hear its horn," Pongo told them, then marched all the other pups after the white cat. The little blue cart was left in the mews at the back of the house—the Cadpig insisted on going into the house and getting her fair share of the revenge.

The white cat took them in through the coal cellar.

"Nothing down here worth wrecking," she said, making for the stairs. Up through the dark house they went, until she paused outside a bolted door.

"Now, if you really can undo that bolt!" she said to Pongo, Goodness knows, *I've* tried often enough."

"Oh, he's splendid at bolts," said Missis proudly.

162

It was a nice chromium bolt, well oiled. It gave Pongo no trouble at all.

There was enough light from the lamps on the Outer Circle to show them a big room in which were many racks of fur coats.

"Why, Cruella must own dozens of them!" thought Missis. And there were many fur stoles, muffs, et cetera, too.

Pongo barked his orders. "Four pups to a coat, two pups to a stole, one pup to a muff. Present teeth! Tear-r-r!!!"

There was not space enough in one room to finish the whole job, so the pups spread themselves throughout the house. After that the fur flew with a vengeance—in every direction. Chinchilla, Sable, Mink, and Beaver, Nutria, Fox, Kolinsky, and many humbler skins—from kitchen to attic the house was filled with a fog of fur. And the white cat did not forget the ermine sheets. She did good work on those herself, moving so fast that it was hard to see which was clawed white ermine and which was clawing white cat.

"I've been slack," she said. "I could have got at these years ago."

"One needs company for a job like this," said Pongo.

"No more furs to tear now," said the Cadpig sadly. She had just shredded a little sable tippet all by herself.

Quiet!" barked Pongo suddenly. Had his ears deceived him? No, there it was again—a distant blast from the loudest motor-horn in England! The next instant, the pups outside barked the alarm.

"Down, down to the coal cellar!" barked Pongo.

There was a wild scurry of pups down the dark stairs. The white cat sprang to a window. "You'll have time," she cried.

"The car's only just turned into the Outer Circle."

But Pongo knew how fast that car could come. And pups were falling over one another in the darkness; there were bumps and yelps. Roly Poly fell through the banisters—it was amazing that he was not hurt. But at last they were all streaming out of the coal cellar into the mews.

"In your places for counting!" barked Pongo. He had long ago invented a quick way of counting the army. Pups formed nine rows of ten, and one row of seven, which included the Cadpig in her cart. Swiftly he counted now. Ninety-three, ninety-four—There were three pups missing!

"They must be somewhere in the house," cried Missis. "We must rescue them!"

Pongo dashed towards the coal cellar—then stopped, gasping with relief. Lucky and the two loud-barked pups were just coming from the front of the house. Pongo had forgotten them in his counting. The army was complete!

"Cruella's nearly here," said Lucky.

"We must make sure she's gone indoors before we march on," said Pongo, and he ran into the narrow passage that led to the Outer Circle.

Missis ran after him. "Be careful, Pongo! She'll see you!"

"Not in this dark passage," said Pongo.

The striped car went by the end of the passage. A light was on inside, and they could see Cruella clearly.

"Oh, Pongo!" wailed Missis. "She's still got her absolutely simple white mink cloak."

Pongo ran on towards the Outer Circle, and Missis ran after him. Cautiously they peered out of the passage and saw the striped car stop in front of the de Vils' house. Mr. de Vil,

who had been driving, helped Cruella out and then went up
the front-door steps. He started to search for his latchkey.
Cruella stood waiting, with the cloak hanging loosely round
her shoulders.

"I shan't sleep if she keeps that cloak," said Missis.

"And you *need* your sleep, Missis," said Pongo.

The same idea had come to both of them. The cloak hung
so loosely, so temptingly! And the relief of getting the pups
safely out of the house had made them feel daring. Pongo was
happy to see his dear wife looking as mischievous as a puppy.

"She'll never recognize us now we're black," he said. "Let's
risk it! Now!"

They dashed towards Cruella and seized the hem of the
cloak. It slipped from her shoulders quite easily—and fell on
top of Pongo and Missis. Blindly they hurled themselves along
the Outer Circle, with the cloak spread out over them and
looking as if it were runing by itself. Cruella screamed. "It's
bewitched! Go after it—quick!"

"No fear!" said Mr. de Vil. "I think an ancestor of yours is
running away with it. You'd better come indoors."

The next moment, he and Cruella started to cough vio-
lently. For as they opened the front door they were met by a
choking cloud of fur.

Somehow Pongo and Missis found their way to the passage,
where they came from under the cloak and dragged it to the
mews. Here the pups pounced on it. And that was the end of
the absolutely simple white mink cloak.

Lights were now flashing on all over the de Vils' house,
and Cruella could be heard shrieking with rage.

"This is where we march home quickly," said Pongo.

Suddenly all her high spirits deserted Missis. Home! But would they be allowed into their home? All her fears came back.

Now they were marching along the Outer Circle again. And now they could see the Dearlys' house ahead of them.

There were lights in the drawing-room window.

"Mr. and Mrs. Dearly haven't gone to bed yet," said Pongo.

Lights were shining up from the kitchen.

"The Nannies are still awake," said Missis. She said it brightly; no one could have guessed how frightened she was, though her heart was thumping so hard that she was afraid Pongo would hear it. Why should the Dearlys let a mob of strange black dogs into the house? And unless they did get in, how could they show the Dearlys they were *not* strange black dogs? Barking would not help. She and Pongo would need to get close to their pets, close enough to put their sooty heads against the Dearlys' knees, or their sooty paws around the Dearlys' necks.

Suppose they were all turned away—ninety-nine hungry Dalmatians, outcasts in the night?

At that moment snow began to fall again, very, very thickly.

166

Who Are These
Strange Black Dogs?

THE Dearlys, the Nannies, and Perdita has spent a sad Christmas Eve. They had all been very kind to each other. Perdita had washed the humans so much that they all had chapped hands and had to use gallons of hand lotion. Fortunately, Perdita quite liked the taste of this.

(She had received no news by way of the Twilight Barking. Reception was bad in that part of Regent's Park—which was why Pongo had done his barking, and listening, from Primrose Hill.)

In the afternoon the Nannies trimmed the Christmas tree. They said it was for Perdita, but they really hoped to cheer the Dearlys up. The Dearlys put Perdita's presents on it, but they had not the heart to get out the presents which they had bought for Pongo, Missis, and fifteen puppies just in case they all came home. Mr. Dearly had guessed that Pongo and Missis were searching for their family, but he now feared that family might be scattered all over England, and the best he really hoped for was that Pongo and Missis might return.

When snow first began to fall, everyone felt worse than ever. "And Missis didn't even take her coat," said Mrs. Dearly. She pictured Pongo and Missis lost, shivering, and starving. So did Mr. Dearly. But they kept the horrid thought to themselves.

In the evening the Dearlys invited the Nannies to come up to the drawing room, and they all played nursery card games: Snap, Beggar-my-Neighbour, and Animal Grab. They all pretended to enjoy themselves, which was very hard work. At last Mr. Dearly said he would put some Christmas carols on the gramophone.

Now, carols are always beautiful, but if you are sad they can make you feel sadder. (There are some people who always find beauty makes them feel sadder, which is a very mysterious thing.) Soon the Dearlys and the Nannies could hardly keep the tears out of their eyes. When Mr. Dearly realized this, he thought, "This must be the last carol we play." It was "Silent Night." Mrs. Dearly put out the lights and drew back the curtains at the tall windows, so that they could see the stars while they listened. And she saw it was snowing again.

She went back to the sofa and stroked Perdita, who, for once, did no washing but just gazed at the falling snow-flakes. The voices singing "Silent Night" were high and clear and peaceful, and not very loud.

Suddenly everyone in the room heard a dog bark.

"That's Pongo," cried Mr. Dearly and dashed to a window.

"That's Missis," cried Mrs. Dearly, hearing a different bark as she too dashed to the window.

They flung the window open wide and stared down through the swirling snow. And then their hearts seemed turned to lead by disappointment.

Down below were two *black* dogs.

Mrs. Dearly said gently, "You shouldn't be out on a night like this. Go home to your owners, my dears."

(She used the word "owners" when she should have said "pets"—that mistake humans so often make.)

The dogs barked again, but Mr. Dearly said, "Home!" very firmly, for he felt sure the dogs lived somewhere near and had been let out for a last run before going to bed. He shut the window, saying to Mrs. Dearly, "Odd-looking dogs. I can't quite recognize the breed."

He did not hear the despairing howl that came from Missis. It had happened, just as she had feared! They were turned away, outcasts in the night.

Pongo had a moment of panic. This was something he had not foreseen. But quickly he pulled himself together. "We must bark again," he said, "and much louder."

"Shall the puppies bark too?" suggested Missis.

The puppies were all lined up out of sight from the window, because Pongo felt that so many dogs at once might come as a bit of a shock. He now said, "No. Only you and I must bark, Missis. And one at a time. Then they will recognize our voices sooner or later. We would recognize theirs, whatever clothes they wore, whatever colour their faces and hands were."

So he barked again, and then Missis barked. They went on and on, taking it in turns.

Up in the drawing room Mrs. Dearly said, "I can't *believe* that's not Pongo and Missis. And look how excited Perdita is!"

It's because we are all so longing to hear them," said Mr. Dearly. "We imagine we do. But there must be something wrong with those black dogs—just listen! Perhaps *they're* lost." And again he opened the window.

Pongo and Missis barked louder than ever and wagged their tails wildly.

"Anyone would think they knew us," said Mr. Dearly. "I shall go down and see if they have collars on. Perhaps I can take them to their homes."

Pongo heard this and said to Missis quickly, "The moment the door opens, dash in and lead the way up to the drawing room. Pups, you follow Missis, noses to tails. I will bring up the rear. And never let there be one moment when Mr. Dearly can close the front door. Once we are *in*, we can *make* them understand."

The front door opened, and out came Mr. Dearly. In shot Missis, closely followed by the Cadpig—now out of her cart— and all her brothers and sisters except Lucky, who insisted on waiting with Pongo. What with the darkness and the whirling snow, Mr. Dearly did not see what was happening until a pup bumped into him in passing (it was Roly Poly—of course). Then he looked down to see what had bumped him and saw a steady stream of black pups going through the front

170

door and the white hall and up the white stairs.

"I'm dreaming this," thought Mr. Dearly and pinched himself hard. But the stream of pups went on and on.

Suddenly there was a hitch. The two pups faithfully dragging the Cadpig's little blue cart, now empty, could not get it up the steps. Mr. Dearly, who could never see a dog in difficulty without helping, at once picked the cart up himself. After seeing the cart, he no longer felt he was dreaming. "These dogs are a troop from a circus," he thought. "But why have they come to *us?*"

A moment later Pongo and Lucky went past and the stream of dogs stopped. Mr. Dearly called into the night, "Any more out there?" To his relief, no dog answered, so he went in and closed the door. Pongo's sooty hindquarters were just rounding the bend of the stairs. Mr. Dearly followed, four steps at a time, still carrying the little blue cart.

The scene in the front drawing room was rather confused. Large as the room was, there was not floor space for all the puppies, so they were jumping onto tables and chairs and piling up on top of one another. There was rather a lot of noise. Mrs. Dearly was just managing to keep on her feet. She had never been frightened of any dog in her life, but she did feel a trifle *startled*. The Nannies had taken refuge on top of the grand piano.

Mr. Dearly took one look through the door, then dashed into the back drawing room and flung open the double doors. A sea of pups surged in. And now that there was a little spare floor space, Pongo barked a command.

"All pups who can find space: Roll! Roll, Missis!" And he himself rolled with a will.

171

The Dearlys stared in utter bewilderment—and then both of them shouted, "Look!"

The white carpet was becoming blacker, the black dogs were becoming whiter—

"It's Pongo!" cried Mr. Dearly.

"It's Missis! cried Mrs. Dearly.

"It's Pongo, Missis, and all their puppies!" cried the Nannies, from the top of the piano.

"It's considerably more than all their puppies,"said Mr. Dearly—just before Pongo forcibly embraced him.

Missis was embracing Mrs. Dearly. And in a corner of the room there was a great deal more embracing. Perdita was going absolutely wild, trying to embrace eight puppies at once. They were her own long-lost family! It had never struck Pongo that they might be among the rescued pups. He had not even noticed their brown spots, becuase he had scarcely seen any of the pups by daylight before they all rolled in the soot. It turned out that Perdita's family was the one that fitted the Cadpig's little blue cart so well and had pulled it so faithfully.

Mr. Dearly had put the cart down in the back drawing room and the Nannies had now got off the piano and gone to look at it.

"That's a child's toy," said Nanny Cook.

"And it's got a name and address on it," said Nanny Butler. And she read out, "Master Tommy Tompkins, Farmer. Dympling, Suffolk."

"Dympling?" said Mrs. Dearly. That's where Cruella de Vil has a country house. She told us about it when we had dinner with her and asked if we'd like to buy it."

And then Mr. Dearly Saw It All. He remembered Cruella's

desire for a Dalmatian fur coat, guessed that she had collected all these pups so that Mr. de Vil could make many such coats.

"You must have the law on her," cried both the Nannies together.

Mr. Dearly said he would think about that after Christmas, but now he must think about feeding the pups—when all the shops were closed. He hurriedly telephoned the Ritz, the Savoy, Claridges, and other rather good hotels and asked them to send page boys along with steaks. The hotels were most anxious to help when they heard that the Missing Dalmatians had come home. "And at least six dozen more than I ever hoped for," said Mr. Dearly—not that he had had time to count the pups.

Nanny Butler said, "They must be bathed first."

Bathed?" gasped Mrs. Dearly. "*All* of them?"

"They can't sleep in their soot," said Nanny Cook firmly. "Nanny Butler and I will work in our bathroom, and you two can work in yours. And how about asking that Splendid Vet and his wife to pop round and bath pups in the laundry?"

So Mr. Dearly rang up the Splendid Vet, who was delighted to be waked up and called out at nearly midnight on Christmas Eve. He and his wife soon arrived.

Mrs. Dearly got out all her best bath salts and bath oils and all the lovely coloured bathtowels given to her as wedding presents. The Nannies lit fires in every room. Then the three bathing teams got to work. Soon the house was filled with steam and the scent of lilac, roses, and jasmine, mixed with the delightful smell of wet dogs. It took less time than you would believe, because five pups were put in a bath at a time. They were then wrapped in pink, blue, yellow, and green towels and carried to blazing fires to dry. Mr. Dearly thoughtfully turned the drawing-room carpet over so that the soot on it would not come off on the clean pups.

By the time the last pup was washed, the steaks were arriving. There were enough for everyone, even the humans—who were by this time pretty hungry. (They had theirs cooked.)

At last the Splendid Vet and his wife went home, and the house settled for the night. Pongo and Missis showed plainly that they wanted to sleep in their own baskets, with their puppies round them on the hearthrug and in armchairs. Perdita took her little lot into the laundry, on a rather good satin eiderdown. The other pups slept all over the house, on beds, sofas, and chairs. The Dearlys and the Nannies managed to keep chairs for themselves—rather hard ones, but they did not mind because they didn't expect to sleep much. They wanted to be on hand in case any pup needed anything in the night.

When all was quiet in the firelit kitchen and their fifteen pups were asleep, Pongo said to Missis, "Do you remember that night we left—how we looked back at this kitchen? Look, now, at your legal collar on its peg, ready for you to wear tomorrow—and your beautiful blue coat."

Missis said, "I am so hardy now that I shall not need the coat. But I shall wear it from vanity."

At that moment they heard a little noise at the window, a little scratching noise. Outside, in the midst of a white blur, were two green eyes. It was Cruella's cat.

Swiftly Pongo let her in.

"Such goings on at the de Vils'!" she said.

Quickly Pongo turned to his wife. "I haven't explained to you yet, Missis. Our friend here told me that if we could get

175

into that bolted room we could destroy Mr. de Vil's whole stock of furs. Cruella made him keep them all there, so that she could wear any she fancied. I hoped we might put an end to his furrier's business. *That* was why I took the risk of going into the de Vils' house—not to be revenged, but to make England Safe for Dalmatians."

"And it's even better than I hoped," said the white cat. "Because it turns out most of the furs weren't paid for. So Mr. De Vil's ruined."

"The poor little man!" said Missis. "I feel quite sorry for him."

"No need to," said the white cat. "He's as bad as Cruella. The only difference is she's strong and bad and he's weak and bad. Anyway, they're going to leave England tomorrow, to get away from their debts."

"Cruella still has her jewels," said Missis regretfully.

"Mostly sham," said the white cat. "And those that aren't will be needed by Mr. de Vil, to start another business abroad. He says he's going to make plastic raincoats."

"Cruella won't look very well in those," said Missis cheerfully.

"She won't look very well in anything," said the cat. "You've heard of people's hair going white in a single night, from shock? That's happened to the black side of her hair. And the white side's gone green—a *horrid* shade. People are going to think it's dyed. Well, I'm glad to have finished with the de Vils."

"But where will you go?" asked Pongo.

The white cat looked surprised. "Go? I shan't *go* anywhere. I've just *come*—here. I'd have come long ago if you dogs hadn't barked—that night your pets gave me a kind sardine. They won't turn me out. I'll pop up and find them now."

Then Pongo and Missis sank into a blissful sleep without a care in the world—except that they did want to know what the Dearlys were going to do with so very many puppies. . . .

And so did the Dearlys!

Those readers who also want to know should read on. Besides, there is a mystery to be cleared up. Most people who are good at arithmetic are likely to think there is a mistake in this book. It is called *The Hundred and One Dalmatians.* Well, Pongo and Missis and Perdita make three. There were ninety-seven Dalmatian pups at Hell Hall, including those belonging to Pongo, Missis, and Perdita. Three and ninety-seven make one hundred. Where, then, is the hundred and oneth Dalmatian?

He *has* been mentioned, but many readers may not remember him. Those who do not will soon be reminded of him. And those who *do* will soon learn more about him. On to the last chapter, if you please!

The Hundred and Oneth Dalmatian

CHRISTMAS DAY at the house in Regent's Park was absolutely wonderful. The rather good hotels sent plenty more steaks, and though there were not, of course, enough presents to go round, the pups were able to play with lots of things in the house which were not intended to be played with (but were played with ever afterwards). The Dearlys took all the pups into the snowy park; Pongo, Missis, and Perdita circling round to make sure none got lost. And at twilight Pongo and Missis firmly led the Dearlys up to the top of Primrose Hill and barked over a Dogdom-wide network. They even managed to get a message through to the gallant old Spaniel, for two dogs from a village five miles from him made a special trip in order

178

to bark to him. (He sent back a message that he and his dear old pet were very well.) Of course, the Dogdom-wide barking was *relayed*. The farthest-away dog Pongo and Missis spoke to direct was the Brigadier-General Great Dane over towards Hampstead, who was in great barking form.

"There is something very mysterious about this barking at twilight," said Mrs. Dearly. "Do you think they are sending messages?"

Mr. Dearly said it was a charming *idea* but—And then he stopped. Was *anything* beyond dogs? Not when he thought of all Pongo and Missis had done. How had they got ninety-seven pups back from Suffolk? Pongo and Missis longed to tell him, but they never could.

As soon as Christmas was over, Mr. Dearly decided to act quickly, for he realized that one hundred Dalmatians were too much for one house in Regent's Park. They were even a bit much for Regent's Park.

First he advertised—in case any of the rightful owners of pups wanted to claim them. But none did—for this reason: Cruella had *bought* all the pups except those stolen from the Dearlys, because it costs a lot to get any expert stealing done these days. (Cruella had paid more to the dog-thieves who stole from the Dearlys than for any litter she had bought.) And naturally, people who had *sold* puppies never thought of them as lost, or did anything more about them. Only one owner turned up, the farmer who had owned Perdita. And he was quite happy to sell her to the Dearlys.

So there was Mr. Dearly, lucky man, with one hundred delightful Dalmatians. He decided he must take a large country house. Happily, he could afford this, as the Government had again got itself into debt and he had again got it out. And this time he had been rewarded by an income to save his income tax on. So he had retired from business—except for being always ready to help the Government with its sums.

One fine day in January, when the snow was all gone, he said to Mrs. Dearly, "Let's drive out to Suffolk and return the little blue cart to Master Tommy Tompkins, and also hunt for a country house. And we'll have a look at the house where the puppies were imprisoned—not that we'll take *that* one."

Mrs. Dearly laughed at such an idea.

They took Pongo and Missis with them, and Lucky came as a stowaway, under a seat—because he wanted to see the Sheepdog again and be made a Captain. (He didn't stay under the seat long, and everyone was delighted to see him when he came out.) When they reached Dympling they went for a walk round the village and met Tommy Tompkins out with the Sheepdog. So the little blue cart was returned then and there—rather a relief to the Dearlys, who wouldn't quite have known what to say to Tommy's parents. They didn't have to say anything to Tommy, as he still wasn't quite talking (though his chuckling noises were at last beginning to sound more like Human than like Dog). The Dearlys saw at once that Pongo, Missis, and Lucky knew the Sheepdog—and the tabby cat that came hurrying up.

"And now we'll find Cruella's house," said Mr. Dearly.

When they got to Hell Hall there was a large notice outside, saying: "For Sale—CHEAP. Owner gone to warm climate." And the gates stood wide open. The house was empty.

(The Baddun brothers were now in jail for assaulting the man who came to take away the television, which had never

180

been paid for. They weren't minding jail much, because meeting so many criminals was almost better than television; and they now had high hopes of one day appearing on "What's My Crime?")

"What a hideous house!" said Mrs. Dearly.

"What a lovely wall!" said Mr. Dearly. One thing had been worrying him. If he took a hundred Dalmatians into the country, how was he to prevent them from running wild? This magnificent wall was just the thing. If only the house were not so hideous!

"Suppose it was painted white," he said, "and the blocked-up windows were put back? There's a lovely pond in front— almost a lake."

Mrs. Dearly shook her head. But when they got into the house and saw the fine, large rooms and imagined them all white instead of red, she began to feel different.

Pongo, Missis, and Lucky raced through the kitchen and larder, remembering all that had happened there. The Dearlys followed them and saw the furnace for the central heating. Then they all went out to the stables.

"These would make fine kennels if they were heated," said Mr. Dearly.

Then he looked up and saw the Folly, and both he and Mrs. Dearly took a fancy to it. And they decided then and there to buy Hell Hall and make it into a beautiful house.

"Here we will found a Dynasty of Dalmatians," said Mr. Dearly.

Missis was insulted. She thought the word meant a nasty din. But Pongo explained that it meant a family that goes on and on.

Mr. Dearly added, "And we'd better start a Dynasty of Dearlys, to look after the Dynasty of Dalmatians." And Mrs. Dearly quite agreed.

The alterations to Hell Hall were quickly made, and one sunny day in early spring a removal van and an extra large double-decker motor-coach stood outside the house in Regent's Park. The van was for the furniture. The coach was for the Dearlys and the Dalmatians. The Nannies had already gone down by car, to open Hell Hall, Nanny Butler driving. She had added a smart chauffeur's cap to her butler's outfit.

Mr. Dearly came out of the house with Pongo and Missis. Mrs. Dearly followed with Perdita, and with the white cat on her shoulder. (The white cat too was to start a Dynasty at Hell Hall. The Dearlys had promised her a white Persian husband.)

Within the next few minutes two surprising things happened. First, just as Missis saw the removal van and said, "Oh, there's a miracle," a Staffordshire Terrier flung itself from the van, said, "Here we are again," to Pongo and Missis, and hurled itself at Mr. Dearly's chest.

"That's a compliment, if you only knew it," said Jim, who was standing by the van.

"That's right," said Bill. "Old Battering Ram's fallen for you."

"And I for him," said Mr. Dearly politely, rising from a sitting position.

Pongo and Missis managed to quieten the Staffordshire before he paid any compliments to Mrs. Dearly. And then the second surprising thing happened. A large car had drawn up, and the people in it were looking at Pongo, Missis, and Perdita with interest. Suddenly there was a wild commotion in the

182

car, and then the door burst open and out sprang a superb liver-spotted Dalmatian. He dashed up to Perdita. It was her long-lost husband.

His name was Prince. The people in the big car were much touched by his faithfulness to Perdita and at once offered him to the Dearlys, saying they would be glad of a good home for him as they were always going abroad and having to leave him in kennels. Prince was delighted. Apart from wanting to be with Perdita, he knew good pets when he saw them.

So the Dalmatians started for Suffolk, one hundred and one strong. They all sat up on the motor-coach seats, looking out of the windows, and many pepole who saw them pass cheered—for there had been so much about them in the papers that they were now quite famous. And many, many dogs lined the route, as word of the journey had gone out by Twilight Barking. The waiting dogs barked their good wishes, and the Dalmatians barked their thanks, so it was rather noisy in the motor-coach. The Dearlys didn't mind. They thought happy barking was a pleasant noise.

Prince was rather shy at first, so Mr. Dearly sat beside him and punched him, in a way some big dogs like to be punched. (The punching needs to be hard enough but not too hard; it must please, not hurt. Mr. Dearly was a highly skilled dog-puncher.) Prince thumped his tail, then suddenly gave Mr. Dearly's ear a playful nip, which was much appreciated. After that, Perdita's handsome husband felt he was completely one of the family.

When the Dalmatians reached the village of Dympling, all the villagers were out to receive them, with the Sheepdog, the tabby cat, and Tommy Tompkins well to the fore. (The cows were lowing a loving welcome from the farm.) Tommy had his little blue cart with him, and the Cadpig felt just a bit envious—but she was happy to know she had grown too strong to need any cart.

The white Persian Cat, who was now a charming creature (kindness makes kind cats), was extremely gracious to the farm-yard tabby. It was the beginning of a firm friendship.

At last the motor-coach drove in through the wide-open gates of Hell Hall. The pond now reflected a snow-white house with muslin curtains at all the windows. The front of the house still seemed like a face and had an expression—but now it was a pleasant expression.

The Nannies were waiting at the open front door. As they came to meet the Dearlys, Nanny Butler said, "Do you know there is a television aerial on the roof of this house?"

And Nanny Cook said, "Seems wasteful not to make use of it."

Then Mr. Dearly knew that the Nannies wished for television in the kitchen and he at once suggested it. Pongo and Missis were delighted, for they knew how very much their smallest daughter had missed it.

But during the many happy hours the Cadpig was to sit watching it in the warm kitchen, she never liked it *quite* so much as that other television—that still, silent television she had seen on Christmas Eve, when the puppies had rested so peacefully in the strange, lofty building. She often remembered that building, and wondered who owned it—someone very kind, she was sure. For in front of every one of the many seats there had been a little carpet-eared, puppy-sized dog-bed.

184